Welcome Back to Ivy Gap

A Poignant Comedy in Two Acts

Ron Osborne

A SAMUEL FRENCH ACTING EDITION

SAMUEL FRENCH

FOUNDED 1830

SAMUELFRENCH.COM
SAMUELFRENCH-LONDON.CO.UK

MUSIC USE NOTE

Licensees are solely responsible for obtaining formal written permission from copyright owners to use copyrighted music in the performance of this play and are strongly cautioned to do so. If no such permission is obtained by the licensee, then the licensee must use only original music that the licensee owns and controls. Licensees are solely responsible and liable for all music clearances and shall indemnify the copyright owners of the play(s) and their licensing agent, Samuel French, against any costs, expenses, losses and liabilities arising from the use of music by licensees. Please contact the appropriate music licensing authority in your territory for the rights to any incidental music.

IMPORTANT BILLING AND CREDIT REQUIREMENTS

If you have obtained performance rights to this title, please refer to your licensing agreement for important billing and credit requirements.

WELCOME BACK TO IVY GAP premiered on the main stage of Barter Theatre, the LORT-member State Theatre of Virginia (Richard Rose, Producing Artistic Director) in Abingdon, VA on May 29, 2014 (44 performances through August 10, 2014). The production was directed by Katy Brown, the set designer was William J. Buck, the costume designer was Kelly Jenkins, the music director was Eugene Wolf, the lighting designer was Andrew Morehouse, the sound designer was Miles Polaski, the stage manger was Cindi A. Raebel. The cast was as follows:

EDITH . . . . .Mary Lucy Bivins

LORETTA . . . . .Anita 'Jo' Lenhart

OLENE . . . . Hannah Ingram

MAE ELLEN . . . . .Tricia Matthews

VERA . . . . .Paris Bradstreet

PASTOR JENNINGS . . . . Nick Koesters

WELCOME BACK TO IVY GAP was subsequently produced by Gem Players in Etowah, TN on August 22 (through September 7, 2014). Gem was the first non-professional theatre to produce the three-play Ivy Gap trilogy *(First Baptist of Ivy Gap, Showtime at First Baptist* and, of course, *Welcome Back to Ivy Gap).* The director was LaMone Rose; the cast was as follows:

EDITH . . . . .Jamie Cline

LORETTA . . . . Virginia Orr

OLENE . . . . Robbie Blakley

MAE ELLEN . . . . Amber Henry

VERA . . . . Elaine Baker

PASTOR JENNINGS . . . . .Alan Perry

CHARACTERS

EDITH ELLINGTON – The take-charge former first lady of the church whose life is about to change – mid-60s.

LORETTA WALKER – A new member who'd like to be someone she's not – early 50s.

OLENE WIFFER – A shapely member whose "infamous" past haunts her future – late 40s.

MAE ELLEN RAFFERTY – The church's organist and choir director who wants a whole lot more – early 50s.

VERA REYNOLDS – A flamboyant influential member who takes no prisoners – mid-60s.

JOSEPH J. JENNINGS – The church's new pastor who's trying to replace a legend – late 40s.

SETTING

The majority of the action takes place in the church's fellowship hall located in a fictional town in east Tennessee; two short scenes – created through the use of lighting, sound and a prop or two – are set in the cemetery that adjoins the church (the cemetery setting should be integrated into the overall set design so that it and the hall are viewable by the audience at times specified in the script). The hall is essentially an open area simply furnished with chairs, tables, a piano and the like. To the rear and open to the space is an elevated stage on which there's a lectern and a pedestal microphone (a set of steps leads to the aforementioned elevated area). A line graph mounted on a tripod (and viewable by the audience) displays the church's progress (or lack of progress) funding renovation of the sanctuary. A door – which opens from the stage and leads to the church's sanctuary – is upstage left; a second door exiting to the cemetery and a parking area is down right. In addition, characters can enter and exit the hall (from a second parking lot) down center using a theatre aisle as access. From the hall, one can look out over the church's expansive lawn.

TIME/SCENES

Early Autumn 1970, five-months following Pastor Ellington's death.

ACT I

Scene I: First Baptist of Ivy Gap's cemetery, a cool morning in September.
Scene II: The church's fellowship hall, several days later, a Sunday afternoon.
Scene III: The fellowship hall, the following day.
Scene IV: The fellowship hall, the following morning.

ACT II

Scene I: The cemetery & fellowship hall, a month later.
Scene II: The fellowship hall, the following afternoon, a Friday.
Scene III: The fellowship hall, the following evening, shortly before the church's gala Texas Night at First Baptist barbecue.

PLAYWRIGHT'S NOTES

WELCOME BACK TO IVY GAP is the third in a series of stand-alone plays set in the fictional First Baptist Church of Ivy Gap. The first two in what is now a trilogy (*FIRST BAPTIST OF IVY GAP* and *SHOWTIME AT FIRST BAPTIST*) were selected as winning entries in a number of major play competitions. Both premiered for extended runs (40-plus performances) on the 508-seat main stage of Barter Theatre, the LORT-member State Theatre of Virginia. They were later published by Samuel French and subsequently produced by hundreds of theatres throughout the U.S. and Canada. One reviewer noted, "Please know that having been to Ivy Gap previously is no requirement for enjoying this hilarious but warm play."

PRODUCTION NOTES

Theatres may want to consider a device used by Barter Theatre that entertained audiences during scene changes. Dressed in 1970s go-to-church attire, stage hands changed the set as necessary, in the process playing out their own little improvised roles, e.g., men – rather than do only their job – sat at a table, pretending to eat from a casserole only to be admonished by the women. The effect added to the audience's enjoyment, while giving behind-the-scene folks a bit of on-stage recognition.

Dedicated to my beautiful sisters-in-law, Peggy Breeland Sledge and Alinda Capps Sledge and my inspiring wife, Melissa Sledge Osborne, whose stories, voices, humor, love, and support shine through these pages.

ACT I

Scene One

(The cemetery of First Baptist Church of Ivy Gap, Tennessee which – for the purposes of the play – is created to one side of the theater's stage through the use of lighting, sound and a prop or two [in actuality, it's just steps from the church]. We see – marked by a tombstone – Pastor Charles W. Ellington's plot. It's a cool September morning, the sky is gray and leaves dot the ground. If we listen carefully, perhaps we hear the whistling of a bird.)

*(At rise, **EDITH** appears. She carries a camp stool. Dressed in a jacket as protection from the cool mid-September weather, she crosses to the plot, picks up a leaf, tosses it aside, looks at the gravestone, forces a smile.)*

EDITH. It's me again, Charlie. Back from Little Rock after looking after Ruth, who's doing as well as we could hope. Thank you, Lord.

(Unfolds the stool, sits.)

I'm gonna sit here now, talk to you without tears running down my face. I'm telling you because I don't want you thinking – a miracle happens, I hold myself together – I miss you any less. That's settled... I've come with news. The new pastor I've been telling you about... Oh, Charlie, from what I've heard, Pastor Joseph J. Jennings is just what First Baptist of Ivy Gap needs. He's a widower. And I suppose that presents some problems. But I'm praying he'll work out fine.

(Beat.)

Charlie, he called me last night. Said he hadn't seen me at church. I didn't tell him why, of course. As hard as it was to stay away, I didn't want him thinking I was looking over his shoulder. Then he did the nicest thing…he invited me to be guest of honor Sunday when they rededicate the sanctuary. I thought about it, wondered how I'd do sitting there, knowing that's where you preached all those years, where that horrible fire started, where you…

(Pause, collects herself.)

I told him I'd be honored. I hope that's okay because I think that's just what I need. I know… I'll walk in that old place, hear Charlie stories…

(Chuckles, recalling a Charlie story.)

Like that crazy morning you baptized the Harrises. First Wanda slips. Then Herb goes down. In a wink, you're down there too. Y'all splashing around like three penguins in a bird bath. That Sunday, Charlie, our baptismal waters truly overfloweth.

(Now laughing.)

I'll laugh like this. And cry some too. But it'll be good to be back someplace I love with folks who've meant so much to both of us. Don't you think? And speaking of them, I've got more news. For the first time in a long time, Mae Ellen's got good things happening in her life…a shiny new Wurlitzer organ and a boyfriend she's serious about. Plus I hear she's behaving herself Sunday mornings…playing the hymns we love the way we love them played. Which is good. And that cute little Ivy Gap girl who put Las Vegas on the map in ways we couldn't talk about? Another miracle… Olene's truly found God. And Vera? Well, she's finally admitting men aren't as evil as she'd like us to think. No miracle. Apparently she decided the morning she and Harry welcomed their first grandchild…a boy. And guess what? They named him Charlie.

(Bravely.)

I know…as much as things change, I'm still that mother hen you told me I was. Happiest when our church is doing well. When dear friends are having healthy grandkids, finding love, finding God. What I hate is not being able to share these things holding your hand. So I'll do the next best thing. I'll keep visiting. Keep sharing news. And I'll do it with a smile. At least I'll try.

(Forcing a broad smile.)

So tell me, Charlie. Is that a deal or what?

*(Silence as **EDITH** stands, bows her head. After a moment, we hear the toll of church bells which continues through the upcoming scene change. Lights on **EDITH** and the cemetery fade to black.)*

End of Scene

Scene Two

(The fellowship hall of the First Baptist Church of Ivy Gap. It's the following Sunday afternoon. The space is set up for a reception to follow the rededication of the church's unseen sanctuary. Hall amenities include a piano, a large table, smaller folding tables [with table cloths], chairs and perhaps a potted plant or two. A line graph positioned on a tripod shows that 60% of the church's $50,000 renovation goal has been reached. On a wall there's a banner; it reads "Welcome to First Baptist of Ivy Gap… Where Saving Souls Is Our Business.")

*(At rise, no one's in the hall. After a moment, **LORETTA** enters. As she does, the bells we've heard through the scene change stop ringing. **LORETTA** – southern to the core – is an attractive, confident busybody dressed in the latest fashion, even if it's not right for a Sunday afternoon reception at a Baptist church. She carries a gaudy purse as well as a covered dish [knowing her, it's made of silver].)*

LORETTA. Yoo-hoo. Anybody here?

(Silence. Checks her watch, then critically.)

Baptists! They are never on time!

*(**EDITH** enters; she also carries a covered dish.)*

I was thinking I had the wrong day or the wrong church or the wrong something.

EDITH. You're expecting the rededication –

LORETTA. And reception to follow.

EDITH. Then good for us. We're where we wanna be.

(Shows her dish, then places it on the serving table.)

Have we met?

LORETTA. Uh-uh. But I know you. You're Edith Ellington. I've heard so many wonderful things about you. Including…if Southern Baptists had saints, there'd be a St. Edith.

EDITH. Thank you, but –

LORETTA. I am so sorry about Pastor Ellington. I'm told he was a terrific preacher and a very special man. Of course, being pastor of the same church in the same little old Southern town thirty-something years, a man would have to walk on water whistling *"Dixie."* Then that awful lightning hitting the steeple, burning the sanctuary…

(Stops just short of saying what happened to Charlie.)

Listen to me carry on. I'm Loretta Walker. I'm sure you've heard of me…

EDITH. Loretta Walker…

LORETTA. The author.

EDITH. Uh-huh…

LORETTA. Originally from Atlanta.

EDITH. I've been away, so –

LORETTA. That explains it! I built – well, my super rich husband did – that big old house on the side of the mountain –

EDITH. Overlooking the golf course?

LORETTA. Yes. Unfortunately.

*(**EDITH** doesn't understand.)*

Long story, short. Harold was dying to sink a hole-in-one. Then he did…and he did.

EDITH. You mean…?

LORETTA. The thirteenth hole. The little old ball went in and the little old man went down. Just as I predicted.

EDITH. How awful.

LORETTA. For golfers I'm told it's a religious experience.

EDITH. Yes, but –

LORETTA. Poor Harold also thought Sunday mornings on the course, shouting, "Oh, God," after every swing, constituted going to church. What I'm trying to tell you is…

(Makes sure no one else is present, then softly.)

I write sassy Southern romance novels.

EDITH. I can't say I read many sassy –

LORETTA. I'll fix that! My library's brimming with my sizzling hot reads. Including number two on the 1968 Atlanta best-sellers list…

(Even more secretively.)

"Passion Under The Palmettos." Of course, back then I was a wild and crazy Methodist.

EDITH. There's a lovely Methodist church down the street.

LORETTA. Don't need it. I converted when I heard there's something in the Bible saying, "When two or more Baptists meet in Thy name, thou shall dine." Speaking of fine Christian cuisine, today I proudly introduce to our very own "church of the covered dish"… Loaves and Fishes tuna casserole

(Ceremoniously holds up her covered dish.)

From *Southern Living.* Along with a guarantee… money back if it doesn't tame a mob of Baptists for whom gluttony is the sin of choice

*(**LORETTA** places her dish on the serving table which is empty except for **EDITH**'s dish.)*

Judging by the little we've gathered so far, it had better.

EDITH. The Lord always provides. My pastor-husband claimed it's because of the eleventh commandment –

LORETTA. I've heard that one too. "Thou shall not go hungry at a Southern Baptist shindig." Of course, I don't believe God used the word "shindig" talking to Moses.

*(**OLENE** – attractive, youthful looking and a wee bit naïve – enters. She also carries a covered dish.)*

OLENE. I'm putting this down…giving you a hug for old-times' sake, Edith Ellington.

*(Places the dish on the table, crosses to **EDITH**, hugs her.)*

EDITH. Olene, you sweet thing. I've missed you more than you know.

OLENE. We were here. Waiting for you to come back.

EDITH. Do y'all know each other?

OLENE. I assure you, Edith…*everybody* knows Loretta.

LORETTA. Just as *everybody* knows *everything* about Olene. Including her little – how shall I say it? – *adventure* in Las Vegas. Isn't that right, Olene?

(**OLENE** *and* **LORETTA** *stare coldly at one another. The awkward silence is abruptly broken by "Swing Low Sweet Chariot"* played softly on the organ in the adjacent sanctuary. The music – played as composed – catches* **EDITH***'s attention, perhaps because she'd like to change the tone in the hall.)*

EDITH. Listen. Mae Ellen's welcoming back me with one my favorites…

(Sings the words to **MAE ELLEN***'s music.)*

SWING LOW, SWEET CHARIOT,
COMIN' FOR TO CARRY ME HOME…

OLENE. Careful, Edith…

EDITH.

I LOOKED OVER JORDAN,
AND WHAT DID I SEE…

(Abruptly, the organ accompaniment becomes a jazzed up version of the spiritual. A shocked **EDITH** *makes an effort to continue to sing along. In the process, she looks and sounds downright silly.)*

A BAND OF ANGELS… COMIN' AFTER ME,
COMIN' FOR TO… CARRY ME HOME.

*(***EDITH***, exasperated and confused, stops singing; however, the organ recital, such as it is, continues for a moment, only louder and more riotous, as if the organist were angry at something or someone.)*

OLENE. *It's not our fault, Mae Ellen!*

*(***VERA***, feisty and flamboyant – the obligatory covered dish in hand – enters as the organ recital ends.)*

---

*Please see Music Use Note on page 3

LORETTA. *(Pointing to the sanctuary, looking at* **EDITH.***)* There's something seriously wrong with that girl!

VERA. Edith! How I've missed you!

(Gives **EDITH** *a quick hug, then holds up her dish.)*

Something exciting and new from *Southern Living*…a heavenly tasting Loaves and Fishes tuna casserole.

*(***LORETTA** *glares at* **VERA.** **VERA** *glares back, then places her version of the casserole alongside* **LORETTA***'s.)*

Quick. Before Mae Ellen gets possessed again. How's your sister, Ruth?

EDITH. I'm just back from Little Rock. We're real hopeful.

VERA. And why not? She's at the top of our prayer list. Okay, Olene. What's not our fault?

OLENE. Nothing.

VERA. Well, something's up. We've got ourselves a dazzling new sanctuary…about to be dedicated by our newly called pastor. May the Lord be with him. For he will need it!

EDITH. What does that mean?

VERA. Remember that brand-spanking, louder-than-ever organ Mae Ellen wanted more than salvation itself?

EDITH. Sure I remember.

VERA. Well, you've just heard it. Yet she's back to being the Mae Ellen you *don't* want to remember –

EDITH. Don't tell me that.

VERA. Nothing to do I suppose with that new boyfriend she's been falling all over?

(Looks at **OLENE** *who looks away.)*

Oh, Lord! They broke up!

(An unhappy **MAE ELLEN** *abruptly enters. She's a mess and her hippie-era attire doesn't help.)*

OLENE. *(Whispering to the others.)* Pretend you don't know.

VERA. I'm not that good of an actress. Well, maybe I am. Big news, Mae Ellen! Yours truly is about to audition for the starring role in our little theatre's production of…close your ears, Edith… Neil Simon's *"Last of the Red Hot Lovers."*

LORETTA. Would you listen, Edith?

VERA. In a month I'll take the stage as the disarming little sexpot who loves cigarettes, whiskey and…

(Under her breath.)

Other women's husbands. Which is something we won't share with our new pastor.

MAE ELLEN. *(Finding her way to* **EDITH**, *without a lot of warmth.)*

I'm glad you're back, Edith.

EDITH. I've missed you more than you know, Mae Ellen. And I'm sorry about…

(Moves her hand to her mouth, knows she's revealed the "secret.")

MAE ELLEN. You told them Reed and I broke up. Didn't you, Olene?

OLENE. Listening to you at the organ… I didn't have to tell them.

MAE ELLEN. Don't stop there! Tell everybody what *you're* planning.

OLENE. I asked you to keep your mouth shut!

MAE ELLEN. She's going into the music business. Isn't that right, Olene?

VERA. With her pretty singing voice… I'm not surprised.

MAE ELLEN. The religious music business!

VERA. Oh, Lord…does God know?

MAE ELLEN. The once-upon-a-time Vegas stripper who showed her *"stuff"* – such as it *was* – to half the men in America wants to be rich and famous –

EDITH. Mae Ellen. Shame on you!

OLENE. *(Also to* **MAE ELLEN**.*)* Why are you doing this?

MAE ELLEN. Instead of doing it by entertaining the devil…

(Perhaps pretending to do a strip tease.)

LORETTA. Now, that's something truly shameful, Edith.

EDITH. Everybody, please…

MAE ELLEN. She's out to win the hearts and minds for God, Jesus and the Holy Ghost with music. At least that's her story.

VERA. You do know, Olene? You've gotta wear clothes to sing *"Holy, Holy, Holy."*

MAE ELLEN. And titty-tassels don't count!

*(**EDITH** and **LORETTA** appear equally horrified at **MAE ELLEN**'s comment.)*

OLENE. Just because I know what I want to do with the rest of my life –

MAE ELLEN. I do too!

OLENE. Well, it won't be as organist and choir director of the First Baptist Church of Ivy Gap.

LORETTA. That's for sure!

EDITH. What are you saying, Olene?

OLENE. You haven't heard? J.J. doesn't like her.

EDITH. Who's J.J.?

OLENE. Joseph Jennings, of course…our new pastor.

EDITH. Now *you're* being disrespectful!

LORETTA. Are you surprised, Edith?

VERA. I don't know that he doesn't like her –

OLENE. Well, I know first hand he doesn't like her organ playing. If that's what you call it. Or the how she dresses or –

MAE ELLEN. Then he's gotta hate that our newest choir member – who sits there Sunday mornings, flirting with him like this sweet little angel she never was – flashed her so-called *"treasure chest"* –

EDITH. *Mae Ellen Rafferty!*

MAE ELLEN. As "Madam Midnight… Las Vegas' infamous… *Queen of the Night!"*

(**MAE ELLEN** *looks at* **OLENE**, *shakes her breasts, storms out of the hall.*)

OLENE. Mae Ellen, come back here…!

LORETTA. (*To* **EDITH**, *looking at* **OLENE** *with disdain.*) Another of my always-right, never-wrong predictions. Madam Midnight will never be in the religious singing business.

(*Upon hearing* **LORETTA**'s *comment, an angry, frustrated* **OLENE** *storms out of the hall. A confused, troubled* **EDITH** *turns to* **VERA**.)

EDITH. What's going on here?

VERA. There's more. Pastor Jennings isn't exactly filling the church.

EDITH. What does that mean?

VERA. It means at ten-thirty Sunday mornings prime seating's available…come on down, grab a pew! Said another way, nobody's confusing him with Billy Graham.

LORETTA. Speak for yourself.

VERA. (*Points to the graph on the tripod.*) Plus pledges to pay fixing up our sanctuary aren't exactly rolling in.

LORETTA. I may be able to do something about that.

(*Pats her purse which we'll soon learn is her signature accessory.*)

VERA. Still, I'll give him a chance…*assuming* he stops fumbling his way through "The Lord's Prayer" –

EDITH. He's new. He's nervous.

LORETTA. Who wouldn't be nervous? A *hippie* at the organ. A *stripper* singing God's music.

VERA. Seeing him bow his head, say in his slow Texas drawl…

(*Slowly in a Texas drawl.*)

"Our F… F… F… Father"…doesn't convince me he knows the maker of heaven and earth on a first-name basis. Of course, that hasn't stopped somebody we know from…

(*Turns to* **LORETTA**.)

Putting on the dog for him Sunday mornings –

(*Pastor* **JENNINGS** *enters, unseen by the others. Among other things, he wears cowboy boots and, of course, carries a covered dish.*)

LORETTA. *How dare you, Vera Reynolds!*

VERA. Dressing up like a big-city Methodist…looking to celebrate the Lord's Supper…sipping who-knows-what from a *plastic shot glass.*

LORETTA. *Well…!*

(**LORETTA** *turns, storms out of the hall via a theatre aisle. As she does,* **VERA** *rolls her eyes, turns, follows* **LORETTA**. **EDITH** *watches, disappointed the things she'd hoped were true, aren't.*)

EDITH. *Well…just… HELL!*

(**EDITH** *sees* **JENNINGS** *[who's heard some of the dissention], raises her hand to her mouth, obviously embarrassed.*)

JENNINGS. Amen!

(*The word – a clue to* **JENNINGS**' *own concerns – is barely out of his mouth when we again hear the roar of* **MAE ELLEN** *at the Wurlitzer, this time playing a very unreligious-sounding rendition of "Onward Christian Soldiers."* With equal despair,* **EDITH** *and* **JENNINGS** *look at one another, then toward the sanctuary as the music comes down and the lights dim to black.*)

End of Scene

---

*Please see Music Use Note on page 3

Scene Three

(The fellowship hall, the following day. A table now occupies the center of the space; several chairs are positioned around it as if the hall were set up for a meeting. Changed too is the graph which shows a dip in the percent of pledges received to date, say to 40%.)

*(At rise, **VERA** is alone in the hall. As she paces across the stage, she holds an acting edition of a play script she's trying to memorize. From time to time we catch a word, but most of the words she utters, she utters to herself. After a moment, **EDITH** enters. Unseen, she watches **VERA** parade across the stage, gesturing and mouthing words in an animated fashion. After a moment, **VERA** sees a troubled **EDITH**.)*

VERA. What if I were to tell you I've got a rendezvous with a forty-seven-year-old owner of a fish restaurant looking for…

(Takes a quick look around, making sure they're alone.)

You know what?

EDITH. Another of your made-up stories –

VERA. In his mama's apartment!

EDITH. Of course, it's a story.

VERA. Where – as red-hot Elaine Navazio – I will flirt, smoke, drink and talk dirty.

(Holding up the script.)

Assuming I remember my lines.

EDITH. Your play!

VERA. Uh-huh. Now sit. Pretend with me…

*(Quickly positioning two chairs alongside one another, then pushing **EDITH** into a seated position in one of them.)*

This is a couch. I'm Elaine Navazio. You're Barney.

EDITH. Barney…?

VERA. Barney Cashman. The fish monger. A. K. A., the "last of the red hot lovers."

(**EDITH** *bolts out of the chair.*)

Edith, I need help!

EDITH. I pretend I'm the "last of the red hot lovers," so will I!

VERA. I can't rehearse at home. Harry'll see me. Play along. Please!

(*Reluctantly,* **EDITH** *sits.* **VERA** *sits next to her, puts her arm around her shoulder;* **EDITH** *again jumps to her feet.*)

EDITH. Oh, no you don't!

VERA. All right! Is this…maybe a wee bit seductive…?

(*Stands, pushes* **EDITH** *back into the chair; then – in an exaggerated fashion – acts out her words.*)

I sashay into Barney's apartment –

EDITH. His mama's apartment.

VERA. Light a Lucky Strike…take a puff…exhale as if I were Lauren Bacall in *"The Big Sleep"*…look at Barney on the couch in a particularly flirtatious way…

(*Looks at* **EDITH** *in "a particularly flirtatious way."*)

Whatdaya think?

EDITH. (*Once again popping up from the chair.*)
I think his mama's gonna come home and spank your bottom. If she doesn't, I will.

VERA. Then ready or not. Four weeks from Friday an unrehearsed Vera Reynolds will appear as a somewhat mature *femme fatale*…known in these parts as an "over-the-hill…hillbilly hussy." Unless our very own "Queen of Southern Smut" gets the role.

EDITH. Tell me you're not talking about Loretta Walker.

VERA. Of course, I am!

EDITH. A fellow Southern Baptist.

VERA. Who's lucky I wasn't handling the immersion.

EDITH. Shame on you!

VERA. The *Queen* says she's written six novels. Hear her talk about 'em, she's spent her life her either rolling in the hay with the entire Soviet army, navy and air force –

EDITH. You can't say that in here –

VERA. Or she's got the filthiest imagination this side of Hollywood. And I swear – and I know I can't do that in here either – they pick her for *"Last of the Red Hot Lovers,"* it's 'cause she's been there, done that!

EDITH. I've been away…way too long.

VERA. Remember what Charlie'd say about folks like her? "A dusty Bible makes a dirty mind." Not only that…she sunbathes on her patio overlooking the eighteenth green wearing you know what…*nothing!*

EDITH. As if you would know.

VERA. A rumor I admit. Until Harry started packing binoculars, calling 'em standard golfing equipment.

(Pretends she's looking through binoculars, likes what she sees.)

EDITH. I come back. Think my prayers have been answered. Find everything falling apart. Including people talking about people in ways they shouldn't.

VERA. Then close your ears because our lustful widow is using husband-number-three's money to weasel her way into our church. Starting with a library she's naming after herself. Imagine her book signings. And speaking of books, reading this…

(Fanning her face with the script.)

I'm getting "you-know-what" all over. And that's something else you can't do in a Baptist Church. What have I gotten myself into?

EDITH. What does Harry think?

VERA. If my husband wasn't chairman of our board of deacons, I'd ask. Another reason to keep my not-so-grand theatrical debut our little secret.

EDITH. Until a month from Friday.

*(**VERA** crosses to exit.)*

EDITH. Where are you going?

VERA. Bible study, of course.

EDITH. *(Smiling broadly.)*
While they'll still have you, huh?

*(**VERA** turns to exit just as **LORETTA** – another colorful purse in hand – enters. They look at one another, hesitate, raise their heads defiantly, then leave and enter, respectively.)*

LORETTA. *(To **EDITH**.)*
I was hoping you'd be here –

EDITH. I'm meeting with Pastor Jennings.

LORETTA. Because I've come to apologize. I let Olene, Mae Ellen and especially that Vera woman's fussin' bring out the worst in me.

EDITH. Actually they've been dear friends for thirty years.

LORETTA. Really? They reminded *me* of girls I met in the Miss Georgia Beauty Pageant.

*(Takes a few pageant-like steps, making sure **EDITH** sees her.)*

EDITH. As a contestant maybe?

LORETTA. I suppose I was. Back when I *would* be caught dead in a bathing suit.

EDITH. How exciting –

LORETTA. – *Until* Miss Macon kept spoiling things. Like yesterday. When these so-called friends spoiled things for you. Speaking of Miss Macon...it wasn't very Southern Baptist of me...but I showed her. I'd tell you. Except you'd think I was horrible or bragging or both.

EDITH. I understand –

LORETTA. I *won*. She didn't even make Miss Congeniality. Of course, I was set on being Miss America. If it hadn't been for the horse, well –

EDITH. Horse?

LORETTA. I also completed in horse jumping events. The animal stumbled. Off I flew like Superwoman –

EDITH. Oh, Lord.

LORETTA. With me went…

(Singing the words.)

"There she goes… Miss America."

EDITH. You didn't get to compete.

LORETTA. But then neither did Miss Macon.

(Pause.)

Now that I've said more than I should about somebody I shouldn't… I've got a heroine to rescue. My newest novel. Tentatively titled… *"Cuddling in the Kudzu."*

(LORETTA *takes* **EDITH***'s hand, smiles, exits. After a moment,* **PASTOR JENNINGS** *enters. He speaks slowly with a Texas drawl.)*

JENNINGS. Mrs. Ellington. Right on time.

EDITH. Edith, please…

JENNINGS. Edith, it'll be. Assuming you'll call me Pastor Joe.

EDITH. Thank you, Pastor…

(Can't bring herself to say "Joe," mumbles something.)

JENNINGS. Edith, are you all right? I'm asking because yesterday – after the reception – some of the congregation got to…f…f…feeling a little under the weather.

EDITH. I'm fine.

JENNINGS. Well, good…good. Do you happen to remember if you ate any of the sweet and sour black-eyed pea salad? Also known as Texas Caviar.

EDITH. I'm not fond of peas, so –

JENNINGS. Uh-huh.

EDITH. Was there something wrong with it?

JENNINGS. It could be somebody added a few too many jalapeños. In Texas, we like our dishes on the frisky side. There, I've admitted it. I fixed it. I brought it.

But before I did, I suppose I added a few too many of those nasty little chilies.

EDITH. Everybody'll recover.

JENNINGS. Sure they will. And once Howard Wilson gets out of the hospital, all will be forgotten. My late wife warned me. She'd say, "I'll make the meals. You say the blessings." Henceforth I'll stay out of the kitchen, concentrate on Amens.

EDITH. Charlie and I had the same deal.

JENNINGS. At church she'd look after things I wasn't good at.

EDITH. Women's programs I bet.

JENNINGS. She'd tease me Edith. Tell me if she'd read the job description, she wouldn't have applied.

EDITH. Wanted…pastor's wife. Must be perfect –

JENNINGS. Able to recite the Bible…backwards –

EDITH. Willing to live in a fishbowl –

JENNINGS. Spend holidays alone –

EDITH. Demanding customers…erratic hours –

JENNINGS. Pay…

JENNINGS.	**EDITH.**
Zero!	Zero!

(**JENNINGS** *and* **EDITH** *share a knowing laugh.*)

JENNINGS. When she passed, I felt lost and alone. The zest I had for church was gone. So one fine Texas day, I submitted my resignation. A month later, I walked away thinking I'd served the Lord long enough.

EDITH. Except you hadn't.

JENNINGS. And God must've known because he gave me another chance. In a part of the country that's as pretty as any…in a lovely town filled with good people who want to serve Him and spread His Word as much as I do.

(*Pause, getting down to business.*)

Edith, I've been here four months. And while some things have gone okay –

EDITH. You were wonderful at the dedication yesterday.

JENNINGS. *You* were there. I *had* to do a good job. It's other areas where I'm… I'll just say it… I'm not connecting.

EDITH. You're being unfair to yourself.

JENNINGS. Attendance is down…pledges to pay off the renovation are being withdrawn…

(Points to the line graph.)

I'd like to hold on. In time maybe hear folks say, "That Pastor from Texas…who almost did us in with jalapenos…he was all right after all."

EDITH. How can I help?

JENNINGS. Just being here, listening to me ramble.

EDITH. What about the women's programs?

JENNING. I don't think I understand…

EDITH. If I looked after some. Long as you know my sister is ill. I may have to leave at the drop of a hat. Also I'm not as young as I was when I followed Charlie around.

JENNINGS. Edith, are you sure?

EDITH. Don't try to talk me out of it.

JENNINGS. Oh, no, ma'am. I wouldn't do that.

EDITH. Something else. When Charlie took over, the congregation didn't fall all over itself accepting him. One of the things that broke the ice was a Saturday night cookout on the lawn. It wasn't always smooth sailing from then on. But something happened that night. So I'm asking…can you barbecue better than you fix Texas Caviar?

JENNINGS. Take me out of the kitchen, I'm the king of the charcoal. Olene told me you were special.

EDITH. Too bad Olene exaggerates. Don't be so hard on yourself. You're doing fine.

*(**EDITH** smiles, takes **JENNINGS**' hand, then turns to exit.)*

JENNINGS. There's something else I should mention…

(**EDITH** *stops, turns to* **JENNINGS.**)

I wouldn't except Olene tells me you and Mae Ellen have a special relationship.

EDITH. The Lord blessed Charlie and me with more than we deserved. One of them wasn't children. We sort of adopted Mae Ellen.

(**MAE ELLEN** *abruptly enters. Unseen, she stands in the doorway, listens.*)

JENNINGS. Then your should know that our board of deacons has concerns about her and her…

EDITH. Her what?

JENNINGS. Her antics on the organ. Her attitude. Especially the way she's been dressing of late.

EDITH. This is a difficult time for her.

JENNINGS. Olene told me.

EDITH. She's been our organist for thirty years.

JENNINGS. I'm just saying there are a half a dozen men looking over her shoulder.

EDITH. They want her to change?

JENNINGS. Yes, ma'am. And I'm not talking out of school telling you they expect it to happen…well…

EDITH. Go on…

JENNINGS. A whole lot sooner than later.

(**MAE ELLEN** *turns to re-enter the sanctuary causing* **JENNINGS** *and* **EDITH** *to turn toward the sound. As they do,* **MAE ELLEN** *re-enters, slamming the door after her. Blackout.*)

End of Scene

Scene Four

(The fellowship hall, the following morning. The space is unchanged from the previous scene with one exception: the piano and bench now occupy a more prominent position in the hall.)

(At rise, an anxious **OLENE** *sits at the piano where she attempts to pick out the spiritual "Give Me That Old-Time Religion."* * *From an earlier scene, we have the idea* **OLENE** *can dance [if only in Las Vegas] and we're about to find out she's got a good singing voice; her piano-playing talent, however, is marginal at best.)*

OLENE. *(Looking up from the piano, cheerfully.)*
Mae Ellen… I need you in here!

*(***OLENE** *again tries to pick out the tune. After a moment, she also sings.)*

GIVE ME THAT OLD-TIME RELIGION,
GIVE ME THAT OLD-TIME RELIGION,
GIVE ME THAT OLD-TIME RELIGION,
IT'S GOOD ENOUGH FOR ME!
IT WAS GOOD FOR THE HEBREW CHILDREN,
IT WAS GOOD FOR THE…

(Stops singing, looks again toward the sanctuary.)

Mae Ellen! You told me you'd help!

*(***MAE ELLEN** *enters. More than in earlier scenes, everything about her – her attire, hair, attitude – is less than what's appropriate in a Baptist church, especially one in Ivy Gap, Tennessee.)*

There you are.

*(***MAE ELLEN** *storms down the steps, crosses to the piano, motions* **OLENE** *away.* **OLENE** *moves as directed.)*

Why are you still fuming at me? I apologized.

---

*Please see Music Use Note on page 3

(**MAE ELLEN** *glares at* **OLENE**, *sits, plays "Give Me That Old-Time Religion."*)

MAE ELLEN. Sing along…come on…*sing!*

OLENE. That's not what I wanna practice!

MAE ELLEN. How about this…?

(**MAE ELLEN** *plays a note or two of a traditional bump and grind tune.*)

OLENE. That's not funny, Mae Ellen!

MAE ELLEN. *(Hits a harsh note on the piano, stops playing, angrily.)*

What do you wanna hear?

OLENE. How many times do I have to tell you I'm sorry?

MAE ELLEN. Reed and I didn't break up, Olene!

OLENE. Then why are you acting like you did? Playing the organ like you're in a beer hall. Wearing that…*that*…?

MAE ELLEN. Wearing that *what?*

OLENE. You're not blind, Mae Ellen.

MAE ELLEN. You're talking about this…?

(*Stands, proudly modeling her inappropriate attire.*)

OLENE. You'd fit right in in San Francisco…

MAE ELLEN. Wonderful!

OLENE. The problem is, this is little old Ivy Gap! It makes you look…

MAE ELLEN. Look what…?

OLENE. Like maybe you don't wanna be here.

(*Pause, then calmly.*)

So you're still together?

MAE ELLEN. He took a job in Knoxville.

OLENE. Okay…

MAE ELLEN. It's done, he'll…come back.

OLENE. And everything'll be okay.

(**MAE ELLEN** – *more hopeful than positive* – *nods.*)

Wonderful! Now here's the music…

(Hands the music to **MAE ELLEN**, *dashes up on to the stage.)*

Promise you'll go with me to Nashville. You can watch the audition. Assuming I live through it – we'll have lunch, shop. It'll be like old times.

(Abruptly **EDITH** *enters.* **OLENE** *sees her, jokingly.)*

Edith can come too.

EDITH. Where am I going?

OLENE. …Nashville… I guess.

EDITH. Is there something happening there I should know about?

OLENE. If I talk about it anymore, it *won't happen.* I'm not saying another word.

EDITH. What won't happen?

OLENE. An audition! That's all I'm saying, Edith!

EDITH. With a record company?

OLENE. …Maybe.

EDITH. A religious record company?

OLENE. They're now called Christian recording labels.

EDITH. When is this happening?

OLENE. Oh, no you don't!

EDITH. How do you expect me to go, if I don't know when I'm going?

OLENE. Tuesday! and you're not invited! And if it doesn't happen. Or I make a fool of myself. It's your fault!

(Loudly into the microphone on the stage.)

And it's nobody else's business!

EDITH. Then we'll seal our lips, say our prayers, rejoice when something wonderful happens. Isn't that right, Mae Ellen?

MAE ELLEN. *(Stands, with the music in hand, takes a step to exit, to* **OLENE**.*)*
Later, Olene.

OLENE. Mae Ellen…!

EDITH. Mae Ellen. Stop!

> (**MAE ELLEN** *stops.*)

> You know when there's something important to be said I've got a bad habit of saying it. So come back here please. Let me say what needs to be said.

MAE ELLEN. Oh, I know what you're gonna say. She does too. Isn't that right, Olene?

EDITH. Then make it easy on us. Tell us what we can do about it.

MAE ELLEN. What would you have me do, Edith?

EDITH. For starters get off your high horse. Quit being a prissy, crabby, difficult fifty-year-old teenager with a crummy attitude who's forgotten how to dress. And something for you, Olene. Think before you say hurtful things to Mae Ellen. Like Sunday. Okay?

OLENE. Okay if I make a suggestion?

MAE ELLEN. Why not, Olene? Since y'all have formed a "Save Mae Ellen" committee.

OLENE. Actually, that's a brilliant idea. Be back in a minute…

> (**OLENE** *dashes down from the stage, out the door leading to the parking lot. The moment* **OLENE** *exits,* **MAE ELLEN** *speaks.*)

MAE ELLEN. You know they're seeing each other.

EDITH. Who?

MAE ELLEN. J.J. and Madam Midnight!

EDITH. It's Pastor Jennings, Mae Ellen…

MAE ELLEN. J.J.! That's what he asked her to call him.

EDITH. I can't imagine they're –

MAE ELLEN. I saw them together! More than once! And they weren't talking about God!

> (**OLENE** *re-enters. She carries hangers holding several dresses.*)

OLENE. Straight from Zippy-Do-Dry cleaners. Whatdaya think, Mae Ellen?

MAE ELLEN. The girl who didn't wear a stitch dancing in Las Vegas wants to dress me. Oh, I don't think so!

(Again turns to exit.)

EDITH. I've spent thirty years looking after you, Mae Ellen! Making excuses for your behavior more times than I care to remember. I won't have that investment wasted 'cause you're currently mad at the world!

*(**MAE ELLEN** stops, but doesn't turn to face **EDITH**.)*

Neither of us can do much about how you feel about yourself. But we can… I'm sorry, I'm gonna say it because I'm no longer the pastor's wife…darn well make sure you don't get fired because you've let yourself go to… *Hell.* Now, come here please…we've got work to do!

*(**MAE ELLEN** doesn't move as directed.)*

If you won't do it for yourself, do it for me.

*(After a long moment, **MAE ELLEN** turns, faces **EDITH**.)*

Okay, Olene. Show us what you've got.

*(As **EDITH** and **OLENE** examine the outfits, **MAE ELLEN** dashes up on to the stage; unseen, she begins unbuttoning her dress.)*

MAE ELLEN. How am I doing, Olene?

*(**MAE ELLEN** has slipped off her dress, revealing a slip. She flings the dress over her head seemingly as a grand finale. Except she isn't through. After a moment, she begins removing her slip, humming appropriate music as she does.)*

EDITH. *Mae Ellen Rafferty! Don't you dare!*

*(**MAE ELLEN** looks at **OLENE** as if to say, "Where do you think I got this idea?")*

OLENE. *(Responding to **MAE ELLEN**'s accusatory look.)* I'll have you know I've kept my clothes on for ten years.

MAE ELLEN. Well, halleluiah!

EDITH. *(Getting the message, looks at* **OLENE.***)*
It's one thing to display your wares in "Sin City." It's another thing to expose yourself in a Southern Baptist Church in the heart of the Bible Belt at ten-thirty on a Tuesday morning.

(Offers the dress she likes to **MAE ELLEN.***)*
Now, come here please. Let's take a look…

(Reluctantly, **MAE ELLEN** *− still on the stage − accepts the dress, holds it in front of her.)*
Don't just stand there…try it on!

*(***MAE ELLEN** *slips on the dress. It's represents a change, but there's lots more work to be done.)*

OLENE. See what these do…

*(***OLENE** *removes her shoes, gives them to* **MAE ELLEN** *who slips them on.)*
Now walk for us…

MAE ELLEN. This is humiliating, Edith.

EDITH. Keep telling yourself…if they didn't love me, they'd be playing bridge. Now walk…please.

*(***MAE ELLEN** *steps across the stage. Her posture is poor, her hair is still too long, her makeup is non-existent.)*

OLENE. Maybe if you stood a little straighter…?

*(***MAE ELLEN** *makes a modest effort to do as* **OLENE** *has asked.)*

EDITH. You can do better than that, Mae Ellen.

OLENE. Your head…hold it high. And don't forget the "girls"…lift 'em up.

(As **MAE ELLEN** *parades across the stage, she cups and lifts her breasts.)*

EDITH. When Charlie was here, I'd see and hear things like that I'd scream, *"Baptist Church… Baptist Church… Baptist Church!"* Now, between my increasingly loose tongue…your former career, Olene… Mae Ellen's organ playing and striptease, such as it was… Loretta's trashy, sexy Southern tell-alls…not to mention Vera's upcoming tryst with somebody I can't tell you about –

OLENE. Tryst…?

EDITH. I formally declare myself…*shock proof.*

> (**VERA** *explodes into the hall wearing a revealing, colorful, tacky, sexy "come-get me" kind of blouse and skirt.* **EDITH** *is surprised and horrified, proving she's not as shock proof as advertised.*)

EDITH. *OH, MY GOD!*

VERA. I hope that means I look like I've got a rendezvous with a forty-seven year old owner of a fish restaurant hoping to make whoopee.

OLENE. Does Harry know?

EDITH. Don't have a stroke, Olene. She's in a play she probably shouldn't be in. Looking at her, I assume she got the role.

VERA. The Queen of Southern Smut is dead. Long live the queen of… Well, I don't know what of. But long may she live.

MAE ELLEN. May I be dismissed, Edith?

EDITH. *Yes! Quickly.* Before you get more ideas on what *not* to wear.

> (**OLENE** *takes* **MAE ELLEN**'s *hand and together they exit through the door leading to the sanctuary.* **EDITH** *studies* **VERA.**)

EDITH. Why are you wearing that here?

VERA. I need to know…is it sexy enough?

EDITH. My idea of sexy is a long flannel nightgown with the top button undone.

VERA. Whadaya think? Really?

EDITH. I think a certain owner of a fish restaurant's isn't gonna have to work hard to get what he's after.

VERA. That makes this hillbilly hussy's day!

EDITH. Do I say "congratulations?"

VERA. Not till I tell Harry, and he lives through it. To get our resident hippe in that, did you have to tie her up or drug her or both?

EDITH. She's a handful. But smart enough to know it's time to change –

VERA. Because Charlie isn't here to protect her –

EDITH. Another reason to miss him, isn't it?

VERA. And our new pastor isn't strong enough to help.

EDITH. He's a good man. In time – let's pray the church gives it to him – he'll be just fine. And if he needs help like Mae Ellen, we're helping. Starting tomorrow.

VERA. In the meantime, we'll pray Mae Ellen sees the light.

EDITH. If she wants to keep her job. Question is…does she want to keep it?

VERA. Which is it, Edith?

(**OLENE** *re-enters, steps to the microphone, then with a flair.*)

OLENE. Ladies and gentle…

(Clears her throat, corrects herself.)

*Ladies…*introducing…the *"new"* Mae Ellen Rafferty…

(All look at the doorway, expecting **MAE ELLEN** *to appear. She doesn't.)*

Mae Ellen…!

(After a long moment, a reluctant **MAE ELLEN** *appears. In* **OLENE***'s dress and shoes – with newly applied make-up and a quick redo of her hair – she looks like a different person.)*

VERA. If I didn't see it myself I wouldn't believe it.

EDITH. You look wonderful, Mae Ellen.

OLENE. Now…if only Mister Reed Hennings could see you, Mae Ellen.

(That's all **MAE ELLEN** *needs to hear to cause her to stand up even straighter. After a moment, she walks*

across the stage, strutting her stuff in a display of renewed confidence, all the while holding her "girls" particularly high.)

EDITH. That a girl, Mae Ellen!

*(As **MAE ELLEN** shows off her new self, **OLENE** – back at the piano – begins picking out and singing "Give Me That Old-Time Religion." After a moment, **VERA** and **EDITH** begin to sing and clap to the music.)*

OLENE.

GIVE ME THAT OLD-TIME RELIGION,
GIVE ME THAT OLD-TIME RELIGION,
GIVE ME THAT OLD-TIME RELIGON,
IT'S GOOD ENOUGH FOR ME!

IT WAS GOOD FOR THE HEBREW CHILDREN,
IT WAS GOOD FOR THE HEBREW CHILDREN,
IT WAS GOOD FOR THE HEBREW CHILDREN,
AND IT'S GOOD ENOUGH FOR ME…

*(With an extra measure of pride, **MAE ELLEN** continues to parade across the stage, her sensual movements contrasting with the words of the hymn. Lights slowly dim to black. As they do the women's live musical performance segues into a recording of "Give Me That Old-Time Religion." It continues through the scene change.)*

End of Scene

Scene Five

(The fellowship hall, the following morning. The piano is back in its original position replaced by the folding table that now sits in the center of the space. The graph shows another dip in pledges.)

*(At rise, **EDITH** and **VERA** are in the hall. As **EDITH** unfolds chairs and places them around the table, **VERA** is speaking. We sense she's in the middle of another of her many stories, some of which may even be true.)*

VERA. So Harry's in bed watching Johnny Carson. Like he does every night before he starts snoring. Then it hits me. If I'm gonna tell him the stink I'm in…that time has come. Unseen, I slip into that dazzling little outfit I modeled yesterday, crawl into bed next to him –

EDITH. If that's true –

VERA. Which isn't easy considering he sleeps on his side and my side of a double bed.

EDITH. – You're telling me more than I wanna know.

VERA. Then – thank you, Lord! – I hit the jackpot. In front of us…in living color on our brand-spanking new seventeen-inch Zenith with Space Command Remote…is the woman Harry would most like to find in his Christmas stocking… *Ann-Margret!* She's flirting with Johnny. And Harry's eating it up –

EDITH. Vera –

VERA. "Harry," I say, whispering into his good ear, "Yours truly is about to appear as a sexpot who's after somebody for something Baptists don't talk about. And, oh – by the way – that *somebody* isn't you. Now, sweetheart, that's all right, isn't it?"

EDITH. – Really, Vera, I know where you're going, so –

VERA. He groans something I take as, "Yes." Then – not wanting any surprises – other than the dandy little one I've got up my sleeve…

(Acting out her words.)

I pop out of bed, slither to the TV. With the push of a button, make little old Miss Ann-Margret disappear. In the process revealing my "come hither" outfit.

(Perhaps **EDITH** *is now fanning herself with her hand.)*

In my most sultry voice ever, I say, "So whatdaya think, big boy? Like my outfit?" I can tell he does because faster than a speeding bullet he's chasing me like *I'm Ann-Margret.*"

EDITH. *Stop!*

VERA. Edith. Please. Harry Reynolds is a Southern Baptist deacon. I can't say any more. Other then I think the play can go on as scheduled. Especially after an extra "rehearsal." If you know what I mean...

EDITH. I walk in here thinking I'll find God. Instead I end up with a tell-all Elizabeth Taylor wannabe.

VERA. I'll take that as a compliment.

EDITH. Well, don't! Now where is everybody?

(Almost on cue, **LORETTA** *enters. Again she carries a covered dish and another in a continuing parade of garish purses.)*

LORETTA. Hmmm...can you smell it?

(Holds up her dish.)

My world-famous Georgia-on-my-mind Brunswick stew. Which remind me of another of my favorite Georgia stories.

*(**VERA** rolls her eyes, looks at* **EDITH**, *which further motivates* **LORETTA**. *to tell her story.)*

There I go again. Start to say something. Stop in the middle. When I know you – and *especially Vera!* – are dying to hear. Once upon a time...how shall I say it?... I had a "moment" with Clark Gable? When I was in the movie, of course.

EDITH. What movie?

LORETTA. *The* movie, Edith! *The* Gone With The Wind movie!

(**VERA** *has heard enough. Steps to exit.*)

LORETTA. Vera, please. I'm not implying little old Vivian Leigh had something to worry about. I was simply a twenty-year old extra – a wee bit on the shapely side – in the scene of scenes…the infamous burning of Atlanta. *Darn that General Sherman!*

(*Perhaps dashing on to the stage, acting out her words which are spoken in an exaggerated Southern accent.*)

Oh, I remember it like yesterday. Rhett leading the blindfolded horse through the flames, Miss Scarlet at the reigns. The director yelling "cut." At which point Clark – covered with soot but looking like…well, like Clark Gable…steps my way, looks at me as if I were Scarlet. Then – heart be still! – he winks one of his bedroom eyes. Oh, I thought I'd died and gone to sugar-daddy heaven.

VERA. Did he kiss you, Loretta?

EDITH. Vera!

VERA. A little peck on the cheek maybe?

LORETTA. I assume, Edith, there's a refrigerator back there somewhere.

(*Picks up her dish, looks threateningly at* **VERA**.)

We don't want any more folks getting sick, do we?

EDITH. This isn't a luncheon meeting.

LORETTA. I know.

(**LORETTA** *gives* **VERA** *another nasty look, exits.*)

VERA. It would almost be worth going to Hell to see that woman sizzling in the devil's kettle.

(*Abruptly, we hear* **MAE ELLEN** *at the organ. As* **VERA** *and* **EDITH**. *listen to a verse or two of "Go Tell It On The Mountain"** played as written,* **OLENE** *enters. When the last note's been played, they look at one another, relieved and pleased.*)

---

*Please see Music Use Note on page 3

EDITH. I believe that's progress of another kind.

> (**MAE ELLEN** *enters. If anything, she looks more polished than in the previous scene.*)

VERA. Sounding good –

OLENE. And looking good, Mae Ellen.

MAE ELLEN. So, you know, Edith… I won't be attending your meeting this morning.

EDITH. May I ask why?

MAE ELLEN. I've got places to go, people to see.

EDITH. Where would these people be?

MAE ELLEN. It won't work, Edith. I know your tricks.

EDITH. Maybe we could come along.

MAE ELLEN. Listen to me, Edith. Nobody's invited!

> (**MAE ELLEN** *smiles a devilish smile, turns, then displaying what she's learned from her make-over lesson, exits.*)

OLENE. Two to one she's hightailing it to Knoxville –

VERA. We can start any time you're ready, Edith.

EDITH. When Loretta gets back.

VERA. You invited *her?*

EDITH. She's new. She's creative. So I did. Plus she needs a friend or two.

VERA. Then you don't need me.

> (**VERA** *stands, looks at* **EDITH** *who doesn't have to say a word to get* **VERA** *to return to table, where she takes a deep breath, sits.*)

EDITH. Thank you.

VERA. At least tell us why you called this get-together.

EDITH. In one of my weaker moments I told Pastor Jennings… I cannot make myself call him Pastor Joe… I told him I'd look after a few of our programs.

OLENE. Sounds like old times.

EDITH. Because I'm allowed to pick and choose, today we're in the party-planning business.

OLENE. *(Acting horrified at* **EDITH**'s *comment.)*
What are you talking about, Edith Ellington? Baptist churches don't have parties. I got that first-hand from the highest authority…

(**OLENE** *and* **VERA** *point to* **EDITH**.)

VERA. Her exact words… "Baptist churches don't have parties…"

OLENE. "Baptist churches have celebrations…"

VERA. "They have gatherings…"

OLENE. "They have revivals…"

OLENE.	VERA.
"They just don't have parties."	"They just don't have parties."

EDITH. *Then we're calling it a barbecue!* Four weeks from Saturday. It's Pastor Jennings' idea. And we're helping. All right?

VERA. F…f…fine.

(**OLENE** *and* **EDITH** *give her a nasty look.*)

Sorry.

(**LORETTA** *re-enters. Crosses to the table.*)

EDITH. I was just saying Pastor Jennings is planning a barbecue –

LORETTA. I love *parties!*

(**JENNINGS** *enters from the sanctuary.*)

JENNINGS. I didn't know y'all were here.

EDITH. Perhaps you could join us?

JENNINGS. Well, sure. Mornin' everybody.

(*"Good mornings" are heard from everyone as* **JENNINGS** *takes a seat between the women.*)

EDITH. We were discussing your barbecue –

JENNINGS. A Texas-style cook-out. Sort of supper on the lawn with a Texas accent.

EDITH. Followed by home-made pecan-praline ice cream in here.

LORETTA. In here? On the lawn? When you can have everything at my little old place? The view from my patio...why you can almost see Texas.

JENNINGS. What a generous offer, Loretta. However, I believe our lawn out there's just what we need.

LORETTA. At least take a gander in that dinky old refrigerator back there. You might come across something with your name on it.

JENNINGS. How thoughtful, Loretta.

(**OLENE** *is steaming at* **LORETTA**.)

EDITH. Perhaps Pastor Jennings could tell us what he'll need from us.

JENNINGS. Well, let's see... I believe I'll need...ahh...

(*A long pause. He's stumped.*)

OLENE. Entertainment.

EDITH. I'm not sure we'll need –

OLENE. What's a party or barbecue or whatever without entertainment?

EDITH. In that case, Olene. You're our illustrious entertainment chairwoman. What else...?

(**EDITH** *looks at* **JENNINGS** *who hasn't a clue "what else?"*)

JENNINGS. Ahhh...let's see...

(*A long silence while trying to come up with something, failing to do so.*)

EDITH. A sign-up list, maybe?

JENNINGS. So we'll know how many people are coming.

EDITH. And who's bringing what.

JENNINGS. Good thinking, Edith. And chances are we'll need a...

(*An even longer pause, stumped more than ever.*)

EDITH. How's this for an idea. We'll put things together for you to consider. You can add, subtract.

JENNINGS. Now that's a plan. Anything else you need from me?

(Silence as the women look at one another.)

Well, then…thank you.

(Smiles, stands, crosses to the door to the sanctuary, exits.)

VERA. A new commandment… "Thou shall not become a pastor, preacher, rabbi – you name it – without having a spouse to pick up the pieces."

(Thinks for a minute.)

Makes you wonder how the Catholics do it, doesn't it?

LORETTA. I know why you've asked us here, Edith. However, we have something far more pressing to discuss than a barbecue.

EDITH. Oh…?

LORETTA. You're aware, of course, that our community theatre – in Ivy Gap, of all places – is about to stage a despicable play titled *"Last of the Red-Hot Lovers."*

EDITH. It isn't despicable –

LORETTA. It is! More important…somebody sitting at this table – who's a member of this church…*whose husband is chairman of our board of deacons* – is playing *the floozy* whose actions make a mockery of everything we believe in!

EDITH. Loretta, please –

LORETTA. *Stand up… Vera Reynolds!*

VERA. *(Stands, ready for battle.)*

I'll do more than stand up –

LORETTA. *There she is…!*

(Points to VERA.*)*

A so-called Southern Baptist intent on showing the world how to corrupt another woman's husband.

EDITH. *Ladies!*

OLENE. Let 'em fight, Edith.

VERA. I have the role *only* because *you* didn't get it!

LORETTA. Oh, I hope you're not implying –

VERA. I'm implying you wanted it worse than I did.

LORETTA. Not true!

VERA. Only problem is you don't know how to act like a trollop…*you only know how to be one!*

(**OLENE** *applauds* **VERA***'s comment.*)

EDITH. *Vera, how awful!*

LORETTA. *Well…!*

VERA. The only thing worst than a trollop is a trollop who's a hypocrite. *Stand up, Loretta Walker!*

EDITH. Both of you! *Stop it!*

VERA. Not only that, Edith…the Loaves and Fishes tuna casserole I brought to the dedication was tons better than hers!

EDITH. You had help. Gabby, remember?

OLENE. Who you'd be lost without.

VERA. I know perfectly well Gabby Williams is the best cook in the county. But *I* brought it!

(*Points first to herself, than to* **LORETTA.**)

She didn't!

EDITH. *(to the audience)* Just what we need. A casserole war.

LORETTA. I assure all of you – *especially you…!*

(*Again points to* **VERA.**)

You haven't heard the last of this! Nor has our board-of-deacons.

(**LORETTA** *storms out of the hall. As she does,* **JENNINGS** *– who's heard the fuss – reenters.*)

JENNINGS. What kind of planning y'all doing in here?

(*Silence.*)

I see…secrets. Which tells me y'all are putting together one heck of a barbecue.

EDITH. I believe we've done enough "putting together" for one morning.

(*Crosses to exit, sneers at* **VERA.**)

You'll excuse me… Pastor Jennings.

(*An angry* **EDITH** *exits.* **VERA** *follows.* **OLENE** *remains.*)

JENNINGS. Should I worry?

OLENE. I'm the one who should worry.

JENNINGS. What are you talking about?

OLENE. An offer to host the barbecue. Home cooking for carry-out.

JENNINGS. Olene…

OLENE. Loretta's got her eyes on you all right.

JENNINGS. I can't imagine.

OLENE. Then you have no imagination!

(*Turns, crosses to exit.*)

JENNINGS. Come back here please.

(**OLENE** *steps back to* **JENNINGS.** *He takes her hand.*)

Did you know, Olene Wiffer? God works in ways I never imagined.

OLENE. Now what are you talking about?

JENNINGS. After all these years – being in love with, then losing a very special lady – I move half-way across the country…find somebody else who makes my heart beat faster. Someone I'm… I'll just say it…falling in love with.

OLENE. Listen to the romantic.

JENNINGS. I'm as backward with women as anybody you know.

OLENE. Not as backward as you think.

JENNINGS. Oh…?

OLENE. Who's holding my hand?

JENNINGS. That's progress, huh?

(*Takes* **OLENE***'s other hand as if to dance.*)

Olene. Do you know how to dance?

OLENE. (*Withdraws her hand, steps away, angrily.*)
Is that some kind of joke?

JENNINGS. Dumb question… I'm sorry.

OLENE. You know why it's dumb?

JENNINGS. I've heard rumors, so –

OLENE. They're not rumors! Once upon a time I *was* a Las Vegas stripper. I danced up a storm. And most of the time I only wore heels! There… I've said it!

(**OLENE** *once again turns to exit. Again* **JENNINGS** *grabs her hand.*)

JENNINGS. Then you got smart. You came home. Rejoined the church. Decided to dedicate your life to God's music. Is that true?

OLENE. The Lord wills it. My audition next week goes okay.

JENNINGS. That's called redemption. It's something we celebrate.

OLENE. By dancing?

JENNINGS. Why not?

OLENE. In a Southern Baptist church?

JENNINGS. Where better to celebrate redemption?

OLENE. Yes. But what if somebody sees us?

JENNINGS. God would approve.

OLENE. What about the board of deacons?

JENNINGS. The dancing I'm talking about…it's not dancing, dancing. It's line dancing. It comes all the way from the Lone Star state.

OLENE. Since I've never been there –

JENNINGS. Then I'll show you.

(*Shows off his line dancing skills. For a Baptist preacher, he's not bad.*)

Whatdaya think?

OLENE. I'd need music.

JENNINGS. Dance with me. I'll sing.

OLENE. I don't think so.

JENNINGS. Nothing to it, Olene…

> (**JENNINGS** *takes* **OLENE**'s *hand, begins to sing, then dance to "Cotton-Eyed Joe,"* *perhaps the most traditional music to accompany line dancing. He dances better than he sings; nevertheless, he's entertaining to all but* **LORETTA** *who has re-entered the hall. Unseen, she watches as* **OLENE** *– hesitant at first – makes an effort to follow* **JENNINGS** *' lead. In wink* **OLENE**'s *pretty much got it and the pair is having a grand old time. After a moment,* **LORETTA** *has seen enough; she turns, angrily retraces her steps, exits the hall.)*

SONG: "COTTON EYED-JOE"

JENNINGS.

> IF IT HADN'T BEEN FOR COTTON-EYED JOE,
> I'D BEEN MARRIED A LONG TIME AGO.
> WHERE DID YOU COME FROM, WHERE DID YOU GO?
> WHERE DID YOU COME FROM COTTON-EYED JOE?
>
> DON'T YOU REMEMBER, DON'T YOU KNOW?
> DON'T YOU REMEMBER, COTTON-EYED JOE?
> COTTON-EYED JOE, COTTON-EYED JOE,
> WHERE DID YOU COME FROM?

OLENE.   **JENNINGS.**

> (**OLENE** *joins* **JENNINGS** *in song.)*
> WHERE DID YOU GO?
> WHERE DID YOU COME FROM?
> WHERE DID YOU GO?
> WHERE DID YOU COME FROM, COTTON-EYED JOE?

JENNINGS.

> WAY BACK YONDER A LONG TIME AGO.
> DADDY HAD A MAN CALLED COTTON-EYED JOE.
> BLEW INTO TOWN ON A TRAVELIN' SHOW.

---

*Please see Music Use Note on page 3

*(***LORETTA** *re-enters the hall, again unseen by* **JENNINGS** *and* **OLENE** *who continue to carry on. In a huff,* **LORETTA** *turns, exits the hall and the church. In her hand is the covered dish intended for* **JENNINGS.**)*

JENNINGS.   **OLENE.**

NOBODY DANCED LIKE COTTON-EYED JOE.
COTTON-EYED JOE, COTTON-EYED JOE.
NOBODY DANCED LIKE COTTON-EYED JOE.

*(***JENNINGS** *and* **OLENE** *continue to sing and dance, unaware their display of mutual affection was viewed by an angry, revenge-seeking* **LORETTA.** *As they carry on lights fade to black, at which point their live rendition of "Cotton-Eyed Joe" segues into a recording of the music, thereby introducing the break between acts.)*

End of Act I

ACT II

Scene One

(The cemetery setting we saw in Act I, Scene I. It's a month after the close of that act, another cool east Tennessee morning.)

*(At rise, we see **EDITH**. She wears a jacket and stands at the foot of Charlie's grave. In one hand, she holds a modest bouquet of flowers; in the other, her folding stool. After a moment, she places the flowers on the grave.)*

EDITH. Here I am again, Charlie. Along with the only flowers left in our garden. It's been so dry. And you know me... I left the watering up to you.

(Unfolds the stool, proceeds to sit.)

First things first. I spoke to Ruth this morning. She won't say she needs me. But I've got this feeling... before I know it...ready or not... I'll be caring for her the way a sister should...full time, without complaining. If that wasn't enough to keep me up at night, there's Mae Ellen who's pulled more shenanigans than Abbott and Costello. But to hear nothing for a month – to miss Sunday services, knowing she's walking on thin ice – what's the girl thinking? But then what was I thinking when I offered to help Pastor Jennings with the barbecue. Which happens to be Saturday night. Oh, Charlie, I've planned and cooked and baked and begged half the women in the church to do the same. Now – except for some decorating and a prayer it doesn't rain – it's up to him. So cross your fingers. He's a good man who needs a little luck.

(Beat.)

And while you're at it, say a prayer for Olene and Vera who I worry about almost as much. Olene's sitting on pins and needles hoping somebody in Nashville liked her audition. And Vera's play opens tomorrow. No matter if Harry and Ivy Gap are ready. Which they're not. Then there's Olene and our pastor making eyes at each other when nobody's looking. Especially me. In the middle of it all we've got Loretta stirring the pot. Never a dull moment in little old Ivy Gap, huh?

(Abruptly serious.)

Except at night when I'm alone in our big old house. I turn on the TV, pick up a book...end up staring into space, thinking about you. Oh, Charlie, I miss you like you don't know.

(Bravely, a wee bit teary-eyed.)

Look at me. After promising I wouldn't feel sorry for myself. The truth is I don't. I had you for forty wonderful years. Which is something to rejoice. And I do. Oh, Charlie – over and over again – I rejoice.

(Lights dim on **EDITH** *and the cemetery, come up on the hall just steps away where* **OLENE**'s *on the stage modeling a particularly garish dress for* **VERA**'s *approval.)*

OLENE. Dora's Dress Shop's been sold. The new owner's having a sale. Ten-percent off. So...tell me. Do you like it?

*(***VERA*** *shrugs as* **EDITH** *– having crossed from the cemetery – enters. She carries a box which we'll learn contains decorations.)*

Edith...?

EDITH. *(Her troubled mind elsewhere.)*
It looks...nice, Olene.

(**EDITH** *puts down the box as* **VERA** *picks up a broom, begins aggressively sweeping the floor.*)

OLENE. What's wrong with y'all?

VERA. I'd be my normal charming small-town self if I hadn't read that awful story in my October *True Crime Detective* magazine.

EDITH. You subscribe to – ?

VERA. Doesn't everybody? This good-looking woman. A real proper, go-to-church Southern Baptist. This tall, hair like mine…

(*Holds her hand out to a height equal to her own, then fluffs her hair.*)

Was done-away-with by her husband for keeping secrets.

OLENE. That is awful.

VERA. Married thirty-five years. Some of it happily even. He goes into a rage. Accuses her of pretending she was the one installing their toilets.

EDITH. Toilets. Oh, come on.

VERA. They went through toilets like we go through toilet paper!

EDITH. She's pulling our legs, Olene.

OLENE. Good. Because I don't understand.

VERA. She concealed the truth. Claimed to be a plumber.

OLENE. But wasn't, huh?

VERA. Didn't even own a wrench. What she did was deceive him.

OLENE. Causing him to…

(*Can't bring herself to say it.*)

He didn't really, did he?

VERA. Not only did he. He got away with it.

(*Speaking to the audience.*)

An all-male jury

EDITH. With all that's going on why are you telling us another of your made-up stories?

(Removes a poster from the box, hands it to **OLENE**, *points to a wall.)*

Over there please.

VERA. Because…unfortunately…it's relevant…

(With dramatics, a sense of great loss.)

Our beloved cook Gabby Williams…*resigned!*

EDITH. And you can't cook!

VERA. I won't say I can't cook. But if I grew tomatoes they'd come up burned, bruised and battered.

EDITH. So…like your made-up plumber who didn't plumb you haven't cooked a meal –

VERA. In twenty years.

EDITH. Which means…

(Looks at **OLENE**, *seemingly gasping at the thought of it all.)*

OLENE. What…?

VERA. Say it, Edith.

EDITH. There'll be blood in the streets of Ivy Gap. Cut the dramatics. What happened?

VERA. Last night, after supper, Gabby tells me she's quitting. Before I can picture my own demise, she's gone. Talk about a last supper.

OLENE. You haven't told Harry.

VERA. Edith, please. Even if he doesn't do me in – before he starves to death – he'll divorce me, then sue me for pretending I knew where the kitchen was.

EDITH. All before he sees you playing house with Barney Cashman –

*(***EDITH***'s criticism impacts* **VERA** *and she shows it.)*

In public.

OLENE. I know what I'd do. I'd hire somebody new.

VERA. Like somebody else in the universe can fix the culinary delicacies that soothe a savage beast named Harry Reynolds. *Gabby's* spicy southern fried chicken, *Gabby's* Carolina sweet potato pie. And yes... *Gabby's* Loaves and Fishes tuna casserole.

*(**LORETTA** sheepishly enters wearing a trench coat, carrying another gaudy oversize bag or purse. **VERA** – and **OLENE** who's out of **LORETTA**'s line of sight – are none to happy to see her.)*

LORETTA. After our little tiff the other day, I wasn't sure I was still welcome.

EDITH. This is a church. Everybody's welcome. Which doesn't mean we approve of things we've been seeing.

LORETTA. Oh, I know what you're saying. And if you're including me, I'll admit it... I overreacted. Now I've got a surprise. Underneath this coat is a brand new dress from Dora's Dress Shop. Soon to be Loretta's Rags to Riches Fashion Emporium. Dora was looking to sell. I bought it! Whatdaya think?

*(With a flair, **LORETTA** removes her coat, revealing a gaudy dress that's a match for **OLENE**'s which **LORETTA** still hasn't seen.)*

Edith. I'm waiting.

EDITH. It's...colorful. And obviously popular.

VERA. Paging Madam Midnight...

*(**VERA** turns to **OLENE** which causes **LORETTA** to do the same. **OLENE** and **LORETTA** are equally horrified they're wearing the same dress.)*

OLENE.	LORETTA.
Oh, good Lord!	Oh, good Lord!

*(**OLENE** remembers **VERA**'s comment, begins removing her dress. **EDITH** sees her.)*

EDITH. Oh, no you don't!

LORETTA. Looks like I'm having a clearance sale... everything twenty-five percent off. Including...

(Turns to **VERA**, *sizes her up.)*

LORETTA. *(cont.)* A dazzling collection of things for the doublewides among us.

(With equal rage, **VERA** *and* **OLENE** *step toward* **LORETTA**. **EDITH** *restrains them at which point,* **VERA** *turns to exit.)*

I've come with more exciting news. I've finalized my culinary contributions to our gala Texas night party, including my spicy southern fried chicken...

*(***VERA*** stops, waits for* **LORRETA** *to continue.)*

My Carolina sweet potato pie. And the *piece de resistance* of the evening. *My* new and *improved... Loaves and Fishes tuna casserole.*

*(***VERA*** charges* **LORETTA**. **EDITH** *can do nothing to stop her.)*

VERA. *GABBY'S Loaves and Fishes casserole!*

EDITH. *Vera... !*

*(***LORETTA*** dashes for safety (perhaps a theatre aisle) with* **VERA** *in pursuit. As* **VERA** *whizzes by* **OLENE**, **OLENE** *hands off the broom.)*

VERA. *SO HELP ME I'LL...*

OLENE. *No prisoners, Vera!*

EDITH. *REMEMBER, Vera... THERE'S ALWAYS...*

*(***VERA*** – shouting and waving the broom above her head – is steps behind* **LORETTA**.)

EDITH. *... TV DINNERS!*

*(***EDITH**, *looking like someone whose world is dissolving before her eyes, watches helplessly from the stage. Blackout.)*

End of Scene

Scene Two

(The hall. The following day, a Friday, late-afternoon. Except for the line graph which shows another dip in pledges, the space is unchanged from the previous scene.)

(At rise, we see **OLENE** *and* **EDITH** *who's doing the only thing she knows to do to maybe make things better, i.e., decorate the hall with items from the box she brought to church in the previous scene. [She and the others — particularly* **VERA** *— decorate the hall through much of this scene.] After a moment, an unusually bubbly* **OLENE** *offers* **EDITH** *a sample of barbecue from a plate she holds.* **EDITH** *accepts and appears impressed. After a moment,* **VERA** *enters via an aisle, waving the newspaper she carries in front of her face as if to disperse smoke from J.J.'s "test" barbecue which we'll soon learn is taking place on the lawn out front.* **VERA** *speaks as she joins* **OLENE** *and* **EDITH**.*)*

VERA. Judging by the smoke out there, our resident Baptist preacher has either torched a tent or elected a pope.

OLENE. He's practicing barbecuing for tomorrow.

EDITH. Making sure everything's set for "Texas Night at First Baptist."

VERA. "Texas Night at First Baptist." Just kinda rolls off the tongue, doesn't it?

OLENE. Edith doesn't want to talk about it. But I've gotta ask…

(Turns to **VERA**, *crossing her fingers.)*

Did you catch her?

EDITH. You're encouraging awful behavior, Olene.

VERA. You know old money bags' been a thorn in my fanny from the beginning.

OLENE. Mine too.

VERA. Yesterday I found something to admire. For a Methodist, turned Southern Baptist, turned home-wrecker who's gonna spend eternity in the smoking section, *that woman can run —*

EDITH. Love your compliments, Vera.

VERA. – *Like the wind.* Long story short. Loretta beats me to her car, jumps in, zooms away at a hundred miles an hour. I jump into mine…fortunately it's Harry's shinny, new, bright-red 350-horsepower turbo-jet Corvette Stingray convertible. In a wink, I'm along side. I'm blowing my horn, shaking my fist. Oh, I am ready to rumble – !

EDITH. Vera…!

VERA. In my rearview mirror – closing like the wind – I see the sheriff and a hundred deputies…their lights flashing, sirens wailing, firing shots wildly into the air…*bang, bang* –

EDITH. *Stop!*

(*An "I've-heard-it-all-before"* **EDITH** *looks at* **VERA** *who collects herself, then calmly.*)

VERA. When I ran out of here yesterday I saw Harry coming in for a meeting. I dropped the broom, hid behind a tree. Then slowly walked to my nine-year old dull-black, four-cylinder Plymouth Valiant two-door coupe. I got in. Drove the speed limit to my friendly, neighborhood Piggle-Wiggly. Where I bought every TV dinner in sight. I went home…found the kitchen… began practicing.

OLENE. Practicing heating TV dinners?

VERA. When you've burnt the first ten, you need all the practice you can get. Edith, sit. You need to hear Loretta's latest.

EDITH. When this place looks like something John Wayne would approve of. Right now we're all about fixing what we can.

OLENE. Until then, take Harry some of this…

(*Offers* **VERA** *a taste of* **JENNINGS**' *barbecue.*)

VERA. I'm Southern to the core, but barbecue…no, ma'am.

(*At* **OLENE**'s *insistence, takes a bite, likes it.*)

Well, now…

OLENE. Not bad, huh?

VERA. Considering it's from somebody who can't be trusted with a jalapeño…amazing.

OLENE. It's the national cuisine of the Republic of Texas.

VERA. There, I'm wrong again. Texas is good for something.

EDITH. Oh, Lord. Don't let him hear that.

OLENE. It's called brisket.

VERA. Guess who she's been talking to.

OLENE. From the animal's chest…

VERA. Uh-huh…

(Chewing more slowly now.)

OLENE. Between the forelegs. Up around here…

*(**OLENE** points to her upper chest. **VERA** stops chewing.)*

Two big clods of muscle and cartilage per cow…

*(Now **VERA**'s all but gagging.)*

Each clod about this big…

(Holds her hands a foot apart.)

EDITH. Olene! We've got the idea.

VERA. *(Spitting the barbecue into a napkin.)*
I knew stuff like this wasn't for me the moment Harry first piled on the charcoal. *Especially* after *I* bought the meat, made the salad, the fixings…all before I forgot how to cook…set the table, lit the fire – bless his heart, he *did* strike the match – brought him a drink, told him the thing was on fire, then sat down to hear folks crown him, "Sir Harry, king of the grill."

EDITH. Maybe you should lay off Sir Harry, considering…

VERA. While *I* was clearing the table, washing the dishes, dumping the trash, the king asked if I'd enjoyed my night off.

OLENE. I would've killed him!

VERA. If the plate had hit him where I aimed, chances are he'd still be around, but nobody'd be calling him daddy. I believe I'm going to be ill.

OLENE. Nooo!

VERA. Nothing to do with the barbecue. Everything to do with tonight.

EDITH. Your play opens.

VERA. Maybe. Maybe not.

EDITH. What does that mean?

VERA. *(Waves off* **EDITH** *'s question, begins helping decorate the hall.)* I know my lines. I should. They've been racing through my mind for weeks. Especially between midnight and six a.m. It's true, Edith… I've been a bastion of this church for decades. Right?

EDITH. You've served on a hundred committees –

OLENE. Sang in the choir –

EDITH. Contributed your time –

VERA. And Harry's money.

EDITH. Which means we'll all know you're acting.

VERA. Edith, please. As a sleazy sexpot, I'm incredibly convincing.

(Thinks about it for a moment.)

But then for six sensuous performances I may be somebody other than who I am –

EDITH. The sassy Elaine Navazio.

VERA. Better than the bored and boring Mrs. Harry Reynolds.

(After a moment.)

I feel better already. I think.

EDITH. Good. Because like it or not, we're still in the party-planning business. And we need help. Including yours, Olene!

(Wistfully.)

I just knew Mae Ellen would walk in here today. Dressed to the "t's," a smile on her face. Tell us things had worked out in Knoxville.

VERA. Mae Ellen's someone else we need to talk about –

OLENE. *(Abruptly, while looking out at the audience and therefore the lawn.)*
Oh, no! It's started to rain!

*(**EDITH** and **VERA** join **OLENE** at the edge of the stage, look out. We hear a crack of thunder.)*

VERA. It's a monsoon!

OLENE. Poor J.J. –

VERA. Looking like Noah –

EDITH. Huddling under his tent –

OLENE. The top of which is filling with water –

VERA. *And just gave way!*

(We hear collective "oh, my!")

That is one wet cowboy wannabe!

*(Another clash of thunder. After which **JENNINGS** runs down an aisle. Among other things, he wears cowboy boots, a ten-gallon hat and an apron. As he steps into the hall, he removes his hat, shakes off the rain. **OLENE** is there to assist.)*

JENNINGS. Being Baptist, you'd think I'd be favorably inclined toward a trickle or two of water.

EDITH. I have it on high authority it won't rain tomorrow night.

JENNINGS. Another worry off my list.

OLENE. Your brisket too. Everybody loves it. Especially Vera.

VERA. Muscle and cartilage are two of my favorite things.

OLENE. Not only that... I've come up with the perfect entertainment...

*(**ALL** look at an excited **OLENE**, expecting her to elaborate on her tease.)*

It's a surprise –

JENNNINGS. In that case, I'll say it again –

OLENE. *(Excitedly, looking at* **JENNINGS.***)*
And you're gonna love it!

JENNINGS. – I couldn't have done any of it – especially the entertainment – without y'all.

(Smiles at **OLENE,** *who smiles back; he exits.)*

VERA. That's for sure!

EDITH. Here we go again.

VERA. He can't help it, Edith. He's a man. There's a big difference between them and us.

OLENE. *(Sensually.)* She's right about that, Edith!

VERA. To prove my point…once upon a time a man was driving down a narrow mountain road as a woman was driving up. As they passed, the lady rolls down her window, shouts, *"Pig."* The guy – who couldn't help himself – angrily yells back, *"Stupid!"* Each of 'em drives on…

EDITH. And the point is…?

VERA. As the guy rounds the next bend, he slams into –

*(***EDITH** *and* **OLENE** *figure out the punch line, announce it in unison with* **VERA.***)*

VERA.	**EDITH.**	**OLENE.**
A pig!	*A pig!*	*A pig!*

VERA. Which tells you all you need to know about the folks who don't listen.

EDITH. Then thank God I'm surrounded by women. Who've got work to do.

(Glances at **OLENE** *who's now on the stage, secretly practicing her line dancing skills.)*

Olene. Are you all right?

OLENE. *(Embarrassed, stops dancing.)*
Uh-huh.

(The moment **EDITH** *looks away,* **OLENE** *line dances her way behind the mike where she hums "Amazing Grace!".* **EDITH** *sees her.)*

EDITH. All right, Olene. What's up?

OLENE. Nothing that's anybody's business…

(After a moment, excitedly.)

Except… I got a phone call this morning!

EDITH. We're listening…

OLENE. From Nashville!

VERA. About your audition!

*(**OLENE** – still behind the mike – smiles, then silence.)*

EDITH. Don't just stand there. Tell us!

OLENE. It's a long story, Edith.

EDITH. Condense it!

OLENE. Y'all know I've been on a few stages in my life, mostly doing things I didn't want my mama to see. Which is something we're not talking about anymore! So you would've thought I'd be okay being on that famous one in Nashville. So what if Roy Acuff, Hank Williams… Patsy Kline entertained there once-upon-a-time?

EDITH. You were in high company.

OLENE. That was the problem. Standing alone – doing a tap dance because my knees were shaking – I kept wondering if it would be more embarrassing to run outta the building before I opened my mouth or to open my mouth, then run outta the building.

VERA. I would've left before I opened my mouth.

EDITH. Ignore her, Olene.

OLENE. Which is when I realized I wanted this more than anything. So I said a quick prayer, took a deep breath, began singing *"Amazing Grace!"* All of a sudden I wasn't scared anymore because the words sounded better than I ever dreamed they would. In a wink, the men listening in their fifty-dollar big-city suits were on their feet applauding like you can't imagine.

(After a moment, almost too good to be true.)

They're sending me a recording contract!

VERA. That's wonderful, Olene!

*(**EDITH** and **VERA** rush to **OLENE**, gives her a big hug.)*

EDITH. Finally some good news. Thank you, Lord!

VERA. Oh, I can see it now. Olene Wiffer…singing hymns on the stage of the Grand Ole Opry.

OLENE. Nobody promised anything about performing big time at the Grand Old Opry. Not right away anyway.

VERA. But you'll be singing hymns?

OLENE. Uh-huh.

VERA. So…if somebody we know made another of her "famous" predictions, claiming Madam Midnight – last time out of my mouth, Olene – would never be in the religious singing business, she's be full of – ?

EDITH. Vera!

OLENE. Yes, ma'am. She'd be full of it all right.

EDITH. Have you told Pastor Jennings?

OLENE. Uh-huh. But I think I'm gonna tell him again!

*(An excited **OLENE** rushes to the door leading to the sanctuary. There she stops, looks back at **EDITH**.)*

First I've gotta ask. Edith, what's it like to be married to a Southern Baptist pastor?

EDITH. Are we hearing more good news?

OLENE. It's for a friend. I mentioned you. She thought maybe you'd have some tips.

EDITH. Since it's a friend.

OLENE. Forget it.

EDITH. Tell her to never learn to play the piano. She does, she'll be playing for every church function for the rest of her life.

OLENE. I don't think I understand.

EDITH. When it comes to pastors' wives, churches operate under the "buy one, get one free" philosophy.

VERA. That was you, Edith.

EDITH. And it's not easy living with a man who works every weekend. Who talks to God and God talks back to. Who knows every members' deepest, darkest secrets and keeps you guessing.

OLENE. *(Discouraged, turns to exit.)*

Now I understand.

EDITH. Most important…tell her she'll end up with a good husband – maybe too good on occasion – and a big, wonderful church family. Take it from me, Olene, there aren't any bigger blessings than that. Okay?

OLENE. Okay!

(Smiles, exits quickly, excitedly.)

VERA. You think…maybe…?

EDITH. Wouldn't that make our day.

(Crosses her fingers, turns to **VERA**, *then seriously.)*

Tell me about Mae Ellen.

VERA. You don't wanna hear.

EDITH. I'm listening…

VERA. The board of deacons met yesterday…

EDITH. Okay…

VERA. They voted… Edith, I'm sorry. They voted to ask Mae Ellen for her resignation. Assuming they can find her.

*(***EDITH** *gasps, sits.)*

I argued with Harry till I was blue in the face. Reminded him how long she'd been here –

EDITH. Thirty years –

VERA. I think our pastor did as well. But when men who think they're something special make up their minds…

(Takes **EDITH***'s hand.)*

I know how much she meant to you and Charlie…

EDITH. First Charlie. Now Mae Ellen…

VERA. And you, Edith. We need you back full time. Not just as a party planner.

(A solemn **EDITH** *nods, then after a moment.)*

Unfortunately, there's more…

(Picks up the newspaper she brought with her.)

Let's see if I can remember the words I've been trying to forget and Harry never wanted to read…courtesy of our once-friendly small-town newspaper…

(Pause.)

"Could it be the *scandalous* play, *"Last of the Red Hot Lovers,"* not only will be appearing soon at a theatre near you…it'll star a prominent member of a local Baptist church…whose husband – tell me it isn't true!"…her words, not mine – "happens to be chairman of the church's *once-*illustrious board of deacons."

*(***EDITH** *and* **VERA** *look at one another, then in unison.)*

EDITH.	**VERA.**
Loretta!	Loretta…!

VERA. Jesus may love her. Everybody else thinks she's a…

(Stops before saying what everybody else thinks.)

EDITH. Harry's furious…

VERA. The chairman of our *"once-*illustrious board of deacons" hasn't been *this* furious since his poodle Fluffy ate the dashboard of his brand-spanking new Mustang convertible. Then it was poor Fluffy…

EDITH. Now it's poor Vera…

VERA. Unless she withdraws from *"Last of the Red Hot Lovers."* Which just happens to open in…

(Looks at her watch.)

Three hours and twenty-seven minutes.

*(***VERA** and **EDITH** *look at one another. Blackout.)*

End of Scene

Scene Three

(The fellowship hall, the following evening, a Saturday, thirty minutes or so before the church's gala Texas night festivities. Tables are now adorned with table cloths topped with vases of yellow roses and an eight-track player is positioned on a smaller table. Also, a number of additional decorative items suggestive of Texas have been added [see "Props" for suggestions]LORETTA. . The line graph has been replaced with a sign; in bold letters, it reads "HOWDY! WELCOME TO TEXAS.")

*(At rise, **EDITH** is alone in the hall where she stands on a ladder in a last-minute effort to add embellishments. As she works, she speaks softly to herself.)*

EDITH. Did you ever think, Charlie, we'd be having a party celebrating Texas at the First Baptist Church of Ivy Gap… *Tennessee?* Speaking of tonight…if there's something you can do. A connection you've got up there to help things down here work out, I know a troubled pastor and pastor's widow who'd be grateful.

(After a reflective moment, her desperation showing.)

Really, Charlie. Where are you when I need you to hold my hand, tell me the things I've prayed for are gonna happen? Because everything's falling apart. Then this morning, Ruth calls from Little Rock –

*(Abruptly, **JENNINGS** enters wearing a western outfit complete with a sheriff's star, holster and toy guns, etc., that would make Hopalong Cassidy envious. Without seeing **EDITH**, he steps to the eight-track, inserts a cartridge. We hear an upbeat instrumental recording of "Deep In The Heart of Texas."*)*

JENNINGS. *(In his own world, singing to the music.)*
"The stars at night…are big and bright… "Deep in the heart…of Texas".

---

*Please see Music Use Note on page 3

(Suddenly **JENNINGS** *sees* **EDITH** *on the ladder. He's more than a little embarrassed.)*

JENNINGS. If I'd known you were up there –

EDITH. Mae Ellen at the Wurlitzer prepared me for anything. Even *"Deep In The Heart of Texas."*

JENNINGS. I thought it might make me feel better about things.

EDITH. I know something that should...

(Points to the lawn area.)

JENNINGS. *(Looking out at the area.)*
Yellow roses on tables.

EDITH. Helium balloons in Texas colors. I thought you'd like that.

JENNINGS. Almost as much as bandanas as napkins.

EDITH. And not a rain drop in sight.

JENNINGS. You've taken care of it all.

EDITH. With help. Including folks out there adding the finishing touches.

JENNINGS. *(Pause, working up the courage to say what must be said.)*
I know you know the board made a decision –

EDITH. It wasn't a surprise.

JENNINGS. Still, I should've been the one to tell you.

EDITH. You spoke up for Mae Ellen. That's what counts.

JENNINGS. If I were half the pastor Charlie was, maybe they would've listened.

EDITH. This isn't about you. It's about Mae Ellen.

JENNINGS. She's gone because I couldn't protect her. Members of the church are at war with each other... I look away. Pledges...they're being withdrawn by the minute.

EDITH. It's not like we don't have some good news.

JENNINGS. Olene's contract. I keep reminding myself.

EDITH. And the best barbecue in Tennessee cooking out there. And maybe Vera's opening night. Assuming there was an opening night... Harry hasn't chased her out of town.

JENNINGS. I called the house –

EDITH. Nobody's home. I know. We'll find out soon enough.

(Senses **JENNINGS** *' despair, takes his hand.)*

Hey, I've got somebody up there working on things. Right now I need to look like I belong at a Texas barbecue.

*(***EDITH*** exits, as* **LORETTA** *– dressed in an outlandish western outfit – enters. She carries a purse and what looks like a cactus.)*

LORETTA. Is this outfit too much?

(Models it, her purse looking very much out of place.)

I hope not. Because I've decided I wanna be an important part of this church. And I'm ready to behave myself, work hard and dress silly to make it happen.

(Holds up the cactus.)

Whatdaya think...?

JENNINGS. A cactus...?

LORETTA. More than a cactus! A memento of Texas that comes with a story. Now where shall I put it...?

(Telling her "story" while searching for the perfect spot to display her cactus.)

It seems my late husband Harold was golfing somewhere near Lubbock. Wherever that is. After embarrassing himself on the course, he had a drink or two too many – he was an Episcopalian, you see. After partaking he took a stroll where those who partake shouldn't tread. Which is where he saw Marilyn Monroe. Being a man he tried to...you know...

(Raising an eyebrow.)

"Whisper in her ear." Too bad the apple of his eye –
the voluptuous Miss Monroe – was an overly endowed
prickly pear cactus –

JENNINGS. The state plant of Texas.

LORETTA. Thus, this little old thing commemorates the
evening the late Harold Norris Walker fell over
backwards trying to "you-know-what to you-know-who"
and got something to remind him of Texas...a pile of
prickly pear needles stuck...

(Whispering.)

Where the Lone Star doesn't shine. Oh, I do hope it's
okay saying that. Right about here...

(Sets the cactus down, admires it.)

Perfect!

*(**EDITH** re-enters, attired in modest western outfit. As she
enters, a particularly anxious **LORETTA** steps to her.)*

I was hoping I'd see you this evening. And I must say I
was so sorry to hear Mae Ellen will no longer be a part
of our church.

EDITH. Are you?

LORETTA. She brought...how do I say it?...a special
"anticipation" to Sunday mornings. And your outfit,
Edith... Dale Evans meets Calamity Jane. How perfect!

*(**VERA** enters, wearing her tacky "Last of the Red Hot
Lovers" costume. She glares at **LORETTA** as the others
glare at her and her outfit.)*

VERA. Of all the people to invite to a party.

EDITH. Of all the things to wear to a barbecue.

*(Abruptly, **OLENE** enters, dressed in her own version
of western attire. She's visibly distressed which everyone
notes.)*

Olene...

JENNINGS. What's wrong, Olene?

*(Silence except for **OLENE**'s gentle weeping.)*

EDITH. We can't help, sweetie, if you won't tell us what's going on.

OLENE. *(Bravely, hesitantly, reluctantly.)*

I got another…telephone call.

JENNINGS. From Nashville?

OLENE. Uh-huh. It seems the one I got yesterday was a mistake.

JENNINGS. You mean – ?

OLENE. I mean the contract offer I had… I don't have it any more.

EDITH. No!

OLENE. They're offering me something else. At least a talent agency is. A real interesting offer I think.

JENNINGS. What is it, Olene?

OLENE. They want to form a female trio. They want me to be part of it.

EDITH. That's good, isn't it?

OLENE. Except we won't be singing in Nashville –

JENNINGS. It's a big country, Olene.

OLENE. And when we sing, we won't be…

(Can't bring herself to say the words.)

We won't be singing hymns. They seem to think hymns wouldn't work so good where they want us to… entertain.

JENNINGS. Where, Olene?

OLENE. Las Vegas. How's that for news, huh?

*(**EDITH** and **JENNINGS** try to comfort a distraught* ***OLENE.*** *At the same time,* **LORETTA** *makes a calculated effort to exit.* **VERA** *sees her, blocks her.* **LORETTA** *sits as directed by* **VERA.***)*

They even have a clever little name for us. Since once-upon-a-time the three of us did the same thing. Introducing… "The Singing Stripper Sisters."

JENNINGS. Olene…

OLENE. We'll dance and we'll sing. While we live up to our name. Just like old times, huh?

(To JENNINGS.*)*

What do you think the board of deacons will think about that?

JENNINGS. It doesn't matter what they think.

OLENE. Oh, but it does!

(Breaking away from JENNINGS, *addressing the others.)*

In case you didn't know. J.J. and I have been seeing each other…almost from the time he got here. And we've become…well, somewhat serious.

JENNINGS. So serious, yesterday I ask Olene to marry me.

EDITH.	VERA.
That's wonderful!	How about that?

(A surprised EDITH *and* VERA *embrace a teary* OLENE.*)*

JENNINGS. She hasn't given me an answer. Have you, Olene?

OLENE. And you know why.

(Bravely to EDITH *and* VERA.*)*

Being a former Las Vegas showgirl doesn't look so good if you want to be the wife of a Southern Baptist pastor and the pastor wants to remain pastor. So I came up with a plan even J.J. didn't know about. I figured if people thought of me as a singer of Christian music no telling what might happen. It might even prove to the Loretta Walkers of the world I'd redeemed myself. The infamous Madam Midnight came home –

JENNINGS. Olene –

OLENE. Found God, fell in love, got married, spent the rest of her life praising Him in song while helping her pastor-husband tend to his church. With luck, doing half the job you did, Edith.

JENNINGS. What Loretta or anyone else thinks isn't important. Neither is whether I want to be pastor.

OLENE. I know you, J.J.

JENNINGS. Listen to me, Olene. I won't be pastor here or anywhere if we don't pay off the renovation. Everything depends on that.

VERA. The board threatened you?

> (**JENNINGS** *doesn't answer, which answers* **VERA***'s question.*)
>
> *Harr…rry!*
>
> (*Abruptly, we hear "The Halleluiah Chorus"** played on the church's organ. After a moment, the beat becomes riotous, ending as abruptly as it began.*)

VERA.	**EDITH.**
Mae Ellen!	She's back!

> (*An elegantly dressed and an extraordinarily refined* **MAE ELLEN** *– high heels and all – enters.* **EDITH** *and* **VERA** *embrace her as* **JENNINGS** *continues to comfort* **OLENE.***)

VERA.	**EDITH.**
Where have you been?	We've been worried sick about you.

JENNINGS. Welcome back, Mae Ellen.

MAE ELLEN. (*Notes the western attire.*)
Y'all are ready for the last roundup I see.

JENNINGS. Tonight's our Texas Night barbecue.

MAE ELLEN. (*Sees* **VERA** *in her "come-hither" outfit.*)
Too bad somebody didn't get the message.

> (*Now looking carefully at* **OLENE.***)

You're crying, Olene. What's wrong?

OLENE. (*Shaking her head, trying to hold back tears.*)
Nothing –

MAE ELLEN. Edith. You're a mess too. What's going on?

> (**JENNINGS, VERA** *and* **EDITH** *defer to* **OLENE.***)

---

*Please see Music Use Note on page 3

OLENE. Nothing…except yesterday I had a recording offer from Nashville. Which I don't have any more.

MAE ELLEN. What happened?

VERA. May I answer that, Olene?

EDITH. What are you saying, Vera?

VERA. We know who wrote the newspaper article, right?

EDITH. About your so-called "scandalous" play.

VERA. And that the "star" of the play was the wife of the chairman of the church's board of deacons. Congratulations, Loretta…you made Harry livid. What we didn't know was she was so determined to publish the article, she bought the newspaper.

MAE ELLEN. How would you know?

VERA. Never embarrass a livid man who knows everybody in town.

EDITH. Oh, Loretta…

VERA. And don't believe for a second, Olene, folks at the record company all of a sudden found out you visited Las Vegas once-upon-a-time.

(**OLENE** *points to* **LORETTA**. **VERA** *nods in return.*)

When somebody wants to destroy dreams so badly she buys a newspaper…nothing's beyond her. Including figuring out who you auditioned with. Then making a phone call.

EDITH. How did she know Olene had an offer?

VERA. *(To* **OLENE.***)*

Did you tell anybody other than us?

OLENE. I think so.

VERA. Who?

OLENE. Everbody.

EDITH. How could you, Loretta?

VERA. There's more. Except I'm sworn to secrecy –

JENNINGS. I'm not. We both know, Loretta, you led the charge against Mae Ellen. Letters, calls to me, members of the board –

MAE ELLEN. Welcome to Loretta's "hit list," Olene.

JENNINGS. Always promising to pay off the renovation –

EDITH. If Mae Ellen were fired.

(Beat.)

Why, Loretta? I don't understand.

LORETTA. Because…

(Cornered, feeling the need to excuse her actions.)

Because this is a church.

JENNINGS. *(After a moment, displaying a Charlie-like level of pastoral passion.)*

Whoa now…are you saying you think of yourself as a modern-day Jonah? God came to you like he did to him? Instead of sending you to the city of Nineveh, he sent you to Ivy Gap to save us from Vera, Mae Ellen and Olene's supposed wickedness? Is that what this is all about?

LORETTA. The people of Nineveh changed. God pardoned the city. The people were saved.

JENNINGS. You set out to save Vera from a role in a Neil Simon comedy.

LORETTA. In which she depicted a tramp who stole others women's husbands.

VERA. Never mind it was a role you wanted for yourself.

JENNINGS. You saved Olene from a career singing Christian music.

LORETTA. As a hypocrite.

JENNINGS. And Mae Ellen from her job as the church's choir director and organist.

LORETTA. Her music was disrespectful to God.

JENNINGS. In the process you saved a church that's been saving souls for a hundred years.

VERA. All this "saving" by somebody who wrote "sassy, Southern romance novels"…including something called *"Passion Under The Palmettos."* Who's going to save you, Loretta?

LORETTA. I…found God.

JENNINGS. And Olene – whose dream was to praise God in song – hasn't? Or Vera who's been a life-long member of the church, all the while teaching Sunday school and caring for the chairman of church's board of deacons. Or Mae Ellen who – until two weeks ago – led our choir and played the organ while attending two services a week for thirty years. They don't know God?

(An embarrassed, defeated **LORETTA** *tries again to do what she wanted to do earlier, exit.)*

EDITH. You need to hear this, Loretta…

*(***LORETTA*** stops, doesn't look back.)*

That awful morning five months ago when we buried Charlie I promised myself – Charlie, too – I'd be a part of this church till y'all buried me. Except for not wanting to be seen looking over our new pastor's shoulder and having to be in Little Rock, I've kept that promise. Which meant I did a lot of praying. Including, Mae Ellen, asking God to help you find whatever it is that'll make you happy. I don't know which of us wanted that more. That you'd live your dream, Olene, singing God's music. I knew how important that was to you. That, Vera…you and Harry would be happy together like all those times you couldn't say his name without a smile on your face. I prayed, too, that our church would come to know what I know…they've hired a good pastor and a good man.

(Looks at **LORETTA.***)*

I prayed for you, too, Loretta…hoping you'd stop playing with other folks lives 'cause that's wrong.

(Beat, then bravely.)

Someday maybe all these good things will happen. If they do it'll be without me celebrating with you. In the morning I'm leaving Ivy Gap.

MAE ELLEN. You can't do that, Edith.

EDITH. Ruth needs me full time.

VERA. You'll come back.

EDITH. At some point, God willing. I wonder what I'll find.

(**EDITH** *and the others look at* **LORETTA** *who's at loss for words. After a moment, she opens her purse, appears to write a check.*)

JENNINGS. If that's what I think it is, Loretta…it's not what God expects from you.

(**LORETTA** *looks up at* **JENNINGS**.)

He expects you to repent. He expects you to change.

(*Silence again as all eyes turn to* **LORETTA** *who body language shows a progression from defensiveness to a willingness to accept responsibility.*)

LORETTA. (*Spoken hesitantly with difficulty.*)

I'm not a writer… I never was. I wasn't Miss Georgia. I never met Clark Gable or any other movie star. What I am is somebody who lived in the shadows of important husbands. They made me feel important. Until they died or divorced me, and I was alone and didn't feel important anymore. To make up for what I'd lost, I began making up stories…telling anybody who'd listen the exciting things I wish I'd done. When that didn't work, I tried using money. Which is when y'all figured me out. I resented it. I got angry. Became somebody who did everything she could to destroy dreams. Tonight – when I saw how badly I hurt you, Olene, how I've hurt all of you – I understood what I've become. I wanted to shout…

(*A genuine expression of contrition.*)

"I'm sorry."

(*Humbled, turns, rushes toward the exit.*)

Then disappear as fast as I could. That time is long overdue…

JENNINGS. Loretta…

(**LORETTA** *stops.*)

The Bible tells us that we all have a capacity for forgiveness. You believe that, Olene.

OLENE. I'm trying…

(**JENNINGS** *look demands more.*)

I'm trying…*real* hard.

JENNINGS. Vera…?

VERA. I guess. But then I also believe in Santa Claus.

(**JENNINGS** *looks at* **VERA,** *like* **OLENE,** *demanding more.*)

Apology accepted…considering I also tell crazy stories and wanted to be somebody I wasn't.

EDITH. The sassy Elaine Navazio.

VERA. What a somebody to be, huh?

(*Embarrassed by her attire – and what it represents – grabs a western hat, puts it on as the best-available disguise.*)

JENNINGS. Edith…?

(**EDITH** *answers by smiling, stepping to* **LORETTA,** *embracing her.*)

Mae Ellen?

MAE ELLEN. Ask me tomorrow.

(**JENNINGS** ' *look demands more.*)

If Olene can try, I suppose I can. Especially considering things have kind of worked out for me.

EDITH. What are you saying, Mae Ellen?

MAE ELLEN. (*Glances at a depressed* **OLENE.**)
This isn't the time…

EDITH. If it's good news, Mae Ellen, it's always the time.

(**OLENE** *looks at* **MAE ELLEN,** *nods her approval to continue.*)

MAE ELLEN. When I left Ivy Gap I went to –

EDITH. Knoxville. We know.

MAE ELLEN. You're wrong. I went to Atlanta.

EDITH. You don't know anybody in Atlanta.

MAE ELLEN. I do now.

VERA. I'm betting his name isn't Reed.

MAE ELLEN. We broke up about the time Olene said we did.

EDITH. So there's somebody new.

MAE ELLEN. And wonderful!

VERA. I love these kind of stories.

MAE ELLEN. Being in Atlanta, I felt like I was flying high. Unfortunately – after a lifetime here – I wasn't sure I had a parachute. Until that first evening walking down Peachtree Street – dressed in my Sunday best and holding my "you-know-whats high" – thank you, Olene! – I caught myself looking at myself in the window of a strange-something called a "boutique."

EDITH. You liked what you saw.

MAE ELLEN. Yes, ma'am! For the first time I believed I could do anything. Including walk by myself – you're not gonna believe this, Edith – into this sleek-looking restaurant with a fancy bar and a dance floor right out of a Fred Astaire-Ginger Rogers' movie. One step through that door...oh, I knew I wasn't in Ivy Gap anymore. Then, of course, I...

OLENE. You what...?

MAE ELLEN. I don't think I should say.

(*Looks at* **JENNINGS**.)

JENNINGS. My ears are closed.

MAE ELLEN. I strolled to the bar, sat down. Acting like I'd done it a hundred times before, I ordered a martini on the rocks with a twist...stirred, not shaken.

VERA. (*Jokingly.*)
You know where you're going, Mae Ellen...?

MAE ELLEN. Hopefully, where they serve martinis on the rocks with a twist...stirred, not shaken.

EDITH. It's one thing, Vera, to order something like that. It's another to –

MAE ELLEN. Down the hatch, Edith. Then with my head buzzing I got blessed. I met Andrew.

VERA. Tell us everything!

MAE ELLEN. Over a wonderful dinner – things I couldn't pronounce and didn't know how to eat – we talked and talked. When they closed, he walked me to my hotel, kissed me on the cheek, walked away. I knew I'd never see him again. But I did. The next night. Then the next day. And everyday since. Too bad there's a problem.

EDITH. Oh, Lord. He's married.

MAE ELLEN. Way bigger than that, Edith. He's Presbyterian.

VERA. First a drink. Then a Presbyterian. What's this world coming to?

MAE ELLEN. What's important is he's available. And he loves me. Edith, I think I found my Charlie.

(A pleased and touched **EDITH** *hugs* **MAE ELLEN**.*)*

VERA. Y'all wanna know why I'm still dressed like this?

EDITH. The rules, Vera. Only good news.

VERA. *"Last of the Red Hot Lovers"* opened last night.

EDITH. Okay…

VERA. I was in it.

EDITH. And…?

VERA. I was sensational! Just ask Harry.

EDITH. He's not livid anymore?

VERA. You can stop worrying about "poor Vera". Harry… does this look familiar…?

(Smiles broadly, seductively.)

Was so blown away by Elaine Navazio, he kidnapped her, escorted her to the super romantic Inn on Blue Mountain. Everything else is secret. But I'll tell you this…his night with Elaine was almost as spectacular as my performance.

EDITH. What about Gabby?

VERA. Gabby who? Harry's discovered there's something more important in life than Loaves and Fishes tuna casserole.

(Raises her eyebrows, smiles her most devilish smile.)

EDITH. God, forgive her…for she knows not where she is.

*(***LORETTA*** tears the check she previously wrote from her checkbook, offers it to* **JENNINGS**. *He hesitates taking it.)*

VERA. *(To* **JENNINGS**.*)*

Take it…!

EDITH. *Quickly!*

JENNINGS. *(Accepts the check, looks at it, joyfully.)*

Our renovation's paid for.

EDITH. *Halleluiah!*

JENNINGS. On behalf of First Baptist Church of Ivy Gap, thank you, Loretta.

EDITH. *(With a sense of amazement.)*

I'm beginning to think my prayers have been answered.

OLENE. Nobody you know is singing hymns in Nashville.

EDITH. Their loss is our gain, sweetie. We've got you to ourselves.

OLENE. A former Las Vegas – ?

VERA. Olene! We love you the way you are.

*(***OLENE*** looks at* **VERA**, *questioning her comment, still concerned about being accepted as the spouse of a pastor.)*

Hey. After last night, the powerful chairman of our illustrious board of deacons owes me big time.

OLENE. Including if I were to…?

(Looks at **JENNINGS**.*)*

VERA. Especially if you were to…

OLENE. In that case…

(To **JENNINGS**, *excitedly.)*

Yes! Yes! YES!

*(***JENNINGS*** and ***OLENE*** *kiss and embrace.)*

MAE ELLEN. Does that mean what I think it does?

EDITH. What do you think, Mae Ellen?

*(***EDITH, VERA, MAE ELLEN*** *congratulate* **OLENE** *and* **JENNINGS.***)*

OLENE. As my matron of honor, Edith. You've gotta come back.

EDITH. Since I know what I'll find…the first chance I have. Of course, it took some help from Loretta.

MAE ELLEN. It's one thing to forgive –

EDITH. I'm not commending anybody. I'm just saying God works in amazing ways.

LORETTA. *(An expression of relief.)*
Thank God, He does.

EDITH. Without those hateful things we wouldn't be planning Olene's wedding to… I'll just say it… Pastor Joe. And Mae Ellen wouldn't have gone to Atlanta.

MAE ELLEN. I can't believe what I'm about to do…

(Steps to **LORETTA** *to embrace her, then remembers it's* **LORETTA.** *manages a brief, distant embrace and a silent "thank you".)*

VERA. And chances are I wouldn't have tried so hard to be Elaine Navazio. In which case, poor Vera *and* poor Harry.

OLENE. And our renovations wouldn't be paid for!

JENNINGS. That's cause for celebration!

OLENE. Mae Ellen, can you give me a "c".

*(***OLENE** *takes a reluctant* **JENNINGS***' hand and they begin to sing and line dance)*

"COTTON-EYED JOE"*

---

*Please see Music Use Note on page 3

OLENE.   **JENNINGS.**

    IF IT HADN'T BEEN FOR COTTON-EYED JOE
    I'D BEEN MARRIED A LONG TIME AGO.
    WHERE DID YOU COME FROM, WHERE DID YOU GO?
    WHERE DID YOU COME FROM COTTON-EYED JOE?
    DON'T YOU REMEMBER, DON'T YOU KNOW,
    DON'T YOU REMEMBER, COTTON-EYED JOE?

OLENE. My turn…

(Sings her original words to the song.)

    WAY BACK YONDER FOUR MONTHS AGO
    IVY GAP GOT A MAN CALLED PASTOR JOE.

VERA. Would you listen…?

OLENE.

    HE BLEW INTO TOWN AND TALKED SO SLOW,
    BUT NOBODY DANCED LIKE PASTOR JOE.
    PASTOR JOE, PASTOR JOE.
    NOBODY DANCED LIKE PASTOR JOE.
    IF IT HADN'T BEEN FOR PASTOR JOE
    THERE WOULD BE NO BARBECUE FOR US TO GO.
    HE CAME FROM TEXAS, HE TALKS SO SLOW.
    HE CAME FROM TEXAS, PASTOR JOE.
    HE BROUGHT THE DANCE, NOW MOVE YOUR TOES.
    FIRST BAPTIST WELCOMES PASTOR JOE.

*(**VERA** and **JENNINGS** join **OLENE** in song and dance. Then wave to **EDITH** and **MAE ELLEN** to join them; **EDITH** hesitates, then grabs **LORETTA**'s arm and together they join the celebration.)*

OLENE, MAE ELLEN, VERA, JENNINGS, EDITH, AND LORETTA.
    IF IT HADN'T BEEN FOR PASTOR JOE
    THERE WOULD BE NO BARBECUE FOR US TO GO.
    HE CAME FROM TEXAS, HE TALKS SO SLOW.
    YOU CAME FROM TEXAS, PASTOR JOE.
    YOU BROUGHT THE DANCE, NOW MOVE YOUR TOES.
    FIRST BAPTIST WELCOMES PASTOR JOE.

*(**OLENE** waves to members of the church who are assembling on the church's expansive lawn.)*

OLENE. What are we waiting for?

JENNINGS. We're a Baptist church. I'm not sure we should —

EDITH. Have fun?

OLENE. Hey, it's not dancing, dancing. It's line dancing. It's a Texas thing. Plus it's officially…

(Looks at her watch, then to the lawn area of the church where we know folks are gathering.)

Texas Night at First Baptist. AND WE'RE THE ENTERTAINMENT!

(JENNINGS nods his approval as OLENE crosses to the eight-track player, inserts a cartridge at which point we hear "Cotton-Eyed Joe" played on a fiddle. OLENE leads all but EDITH to the edge of the stage where they sing and dance with even greater gusto.)

OLENE, JENNINGS, MAE ELLEN, LORETTA, AND VERA.
WAY BACK YONDER FOUR MONTHS AGO,
IVY GAP GOT A MAN CALLED PASTOR JOE.
HE BLEW INTO TOWN AND TALKED SO SLOW
BUT NOBODY DANCED LIKE PASTOR JOE.
PASTOR JOE, PASTOR JOE.
NOBODY DANCED LIKE PASTOR JOE.

(Singing, dancing, clapping, they remain at the end of the stage [or slowly make their way up the theatre aisle].
EDITH *– watching the festivities from the stage – quietly removes a yellow rose from a vase, steps to the door leading to the cemetery, exits [at which point lights in the hall and theatre dim a bit]. Seconds later a light comes up on the cemetery. There we see* **EDITH** *standing alone at Charlie's grave where she places the rose on the plot. While we can't hear her words over the celebration that continues in the hall [or aisle], we know she's telling the love of her life the good things that have happened to the important folks in their lives. After a long moment, lights on her – and the balance of the set and aisle – slowly*

*fade to black. As they do, perhaps we hear an up-tempo instrumental recording of "Cotton-Eyed Joe."**)

End of Play

---

* Please see Music Use Note on page 3

PROPERTY LIST

Tree leaves
Camp stool
Grave stone
Piano
Tables/table cltohs
Chairs (four or more)
Potted plant(s)
Banner (*"Welcome to First Baptist Of Ivy Gap... Where Saving Souls is our Business"*)
Covered dishes (four, one silver)
Loretta's garish purses (4)
Play script
Sheet music
Pair of matching dresses
Dresses on hangers (two)
Sign displaying progress funding renovation
Eight-track player and tape
Broom
Plastic fork
Newspaper
Western hats
Toy guns
Western belt
Holster(s)
Sheriff's Star
Yellow roses (four)
Various western decorations
Pedestal microphone
Cactus replica
Ladder
BBQ tools
Checkbook & check
Trench coat
Cooking apron
Bouquet of flowers
Vases for tables
Tripod
Sign reading, *"Howdy! Welcome To Texas"*

See script for additional specific clothing suggestions. Western decorations might include Texas state flag(s), cutouts of western scenes, burnt orange streamers, wanted posters, etc.

MUSIC/SOUND EFFECTS

Church bells

Bird sounds

A clap or two of thunder

*"Swing Low Sweet Chariot"**

*"Onward Christian Soldiers"**

*"Give Me That Old-Time Religion"***

*"Go Tell It On The Mountain"**

*"Cotton-Eyed Joe"***

"Deep In The Heart of Texas" (Instrumental) ***

"Cotton-Eyed Joe" (Fiddle Version) ***

*"The Halleluiah Chorus"**

* Recording of organ music supposedly played live by Mae
** Recording suggested for scene/act changes
*** Recording used within a scene